The Boy Who
Belonged to the Sea

Also by Denis Thériault

The Peculiar Life of a Lonely Postman

The Postman's Fiancée

The Boy Who
Belonged to the Sea

Denis Thériault

*Translated from the French by
Liedewy Hawke*

ONEWORLD

A Oneworld Book

First published in North America, Great Britain and Australia as
The Boy Who Belonged to the Sea by Oneworld Publications, 2018

Originally published in French as *L'Iguane* by Éditions XYZ,
Montréal, in 2001, and in English in Canada as *The Iguana*, 2003

Copyright © Éditions XYZ and Denis Thériault, 2001
Translation Copyright © Liedewy Hawke, 2003, 2018

This edition published by agreement with
Allied Authors Agency, Belgium

The moral right of Denis Thériault to be identified as the
Author of this work has been asserted by him in accordance
with the Copyright, Designs, and Patents Act 1988

This is a work of fiction. Names, characters, places, and incidents
are either the product of the author's imagination or are used
fictitiously, and any resemblance to actual persons, living or dead,
businesses, companies, events or locales is entirely coincidental.

Trade paperback ISBN 978-1-78607-335-8
eBook ISBN 978-1-78607-336-5

Typeset by Divaddict Publishing Solutions Ltd.
Printed and bound in Great Britain by Clays Ltd, St Ives plc

Oneworld Publications
10 Bloomsbury Street
London WC1B 3SR
England

Stay up to date with the latest books,
special offers, and exclusive content from
Oneworld with our newsletter

Sign up on our website
oneworld-publications.com

MIX
Paper from
responsible sources
FSC® C018072

To Hélène and Camille.
If it weren't for them, I'd be a wanderer.

1

During a deep dive, a euphoric state resembling alcohol intoxication may occur. Known as 'rapture of the deep,' this phenomenon is due to the narcotic effect of inert gases on the nervous system, brought about by the increase in pressure.

The gulls emerge from the east and gather in crowded clusters on the crests of all the rooftops to wail in unison. They call and answer one another, provoke each other, they scream like witches at a midnight revel, and since my bedroom is upstairs, in the attic, I can hear them tramping about. It sounds as though a battalion of gnomes were manoeuvring above my head. At the window, I see them lined up on the top of the shed like living bowling pins. Sometimes there are so many you'd think you were in an old movie about crazed birds, but, unlike what goes on in Hollywood, our gulls remain harmless. There's no risk of their bills suddenly digging into our caps. Even the garbage bin doesn't interest them. It's like that every morning. To what, I wonder, do we owe this faithful attendance at first light?

I have nothing against gulls, but their raucous dawn serenades annoy Grandfather. It wakes him up, while he's made a tradition out of sleeping late. He'll come out of the house in his pajamas and try to disperse the web-footed little devils by pelting them with stones, but his aim isn't very good, so all he manages to do is amplify the chorus of outraged protests — when he doesn't break a window, that is. If it were up to him, he would slaughter the disagreeable feathered creatures with his Winchester, but Grandmother hides the bullets. She refuses to be part of such a massacre of innocent birds, so we put up with the shrieking until the gulls themselves get sick of it, at about seven, and suddenly fly away all at the same time.

To tell the truth, this commotion, this early rising, suits me just fine. It drives away the night and its icy mists of fear. It lets me enjoy my May mornings, feast on the special light that fringes the sky at daybreak in the springtime. When the gulls arrive, I go down onto the shore, right up to the cathodic hiss of the languid water. I love to see the sky glow red when a flaming, brand new sun blasts across the horizon, proudly surfacing once again at the end of its sombre journey. This is the time to investigate the previous night's underwater events and discover the evidence — simple surprises, sometimes dead ones — the tide has surrendered. The other day, in front of Madame Papet's place, they found a washed-up basking shark the length of a house, with jaws so huge it could have swallowed me whole without even noticing, like plankton. The men scratched their heads at the sight of the enormous carcass. They argued back and forth, wondered what to do with it; they couldn't leave it there because it was obviously causing an obstruction, and also because of the smell which had already begun to rise. While they started to cut it up with a chain saw, some guys from Fisheries and Oceans turned up to record this wreck on land. They stopped the work and took photographs just like police inspectors. All that was missing was the tape, that yellow thing they put up to decorate a crime. I thought they were going to take our fingerprints while they were at it, but they didn't after all; we weren't suspicious enough. After the photographs, the government people sent for a crane and a truck to haul the shark away. I don't know where to. The morgue? A museum? The dump? More likely to the Department of Oceanic Affairs, I suppose, where they'd put it away in a cartilaginous folder. Or in a very large — previously deodorized — file thirteen.

I wonder what that shark died of. It had no injuries, wasn't tangled up in any net. Some shark disease? A maritime problem? A tsunami? An over-powering wave of melancholy? What is the lifespan of a shark, anyway?

* * *

In spite of the gulls, I'm never the first one to arrive on the beach. There's always that other kid who's ahead of me — Luc Bezeau, with that mug of his that reminds me of a radiation victim from the other side of the world, with his Newfie boots, his gawky clown-like walk, and that cap emblazoned with the crest of a heavy-machinery company, incongruously topping his worrisome scrawniness. He comes from the west, dragging along his garbage bag like a janitor as he combs the shore. He collects the empty bottles from around fires lit the previous night by careless fishermen looking for caplins or by other passing gypsies. In a satchel, he gathers empty shells of shellfish, crab backs, feathers, and bits of whalebone. In the beginning, I took him for some sort of environmentalist, but I changed my mind when I saw him leave in his wake all other types of waste. Rain or shine, he turns up every morning, as if that were his mission, except on Sundays, for he has religious obligations on that day. He serves mass at the village church, and since I go there with Grandmother, I can see him orbiting Father Loiselle, that gaseous giant, like some dusky dwarf. Luc makes a peculiar altar boy. With his heavy boots sticking out beneath the skimpy white vestment, with that air he has of a gag that fell flat, his Hawaiian mop of jet-black hair, and especially that faraway look in his almond eyes — those strange X-ray eyes he aims at you as if to see right through you — you'd think he'd just disembarked from a UFO or stepped out of a dryer, but that doesn't stop him from performing his functions expertly. He officiates with a pope-like solemnity. Priestly, scratching himself occasionally — but always unobtrusively — he stands close to the altar like a kind of liturgical watchdog and anticipates Father Loiselle's every gesture. It's as if he were directing the service by remote control. During the sermon, he stands at attention, his arms protruding from his too-short sleeves, yet he remains vigilant, prepared to jump in, ready to spring into action and, all along, only his fingers will move, wriggle, bend, and unbend. If he were to be dropped down on the main street of Dodge City with a Stetson on his head, he might easily be taken for a crack shot at the crucial moment of a confrontation. The desperado of the beaches. The guy who draws his altar cruet before his shadow has a chance to catch up with him. The fastest jingler in the West. I must admit he impresses me with his shy-sponge-like austerity. That face he has of an explorer of the beyond matches my gloomy mood and arouses my curiosity. If he let me, I would definitely try to befriend him, or at the very least say hello to him on the beach when he comes ambling along at the crack of dawn, but that's impossible because he's opposed to such familiarities. As soon as he sees me slouching about near the flagpole or on the verandah gobbling up a chocogrunt, he hurries away without even looking at me. Could he be terribly shy? Or is he perhaps too sensitive to the aura of tragedy that emanates from me? In any case, he gives me a wide berth, the way

Ulysses steered clear of certain notorious corners of the Aegean. He still walks by our house because he has no choice, but furtively, without stopping, and always scuttles away, shadowed by a fear I simply can't understand.

2

Papa suffered from snowmobilitis, a common malady above the fiftieth parallel, what with the north pressing down on you and winter somehow or other needing to be tamed. In most cases, the symptoms abate when spring arrives, but with Papa the illness was chronic, chronological even, and incurable. It was a passion that withstood the therapeutic heat of summer — a latent fever, stirred up by strong October winds and set truly ablaze by the blessed first snowfall. Snowmobiling was something Papa couldn't get enough of. He could have slept on his beloved machine and, come to think of it, he must have dozed off a lot as a baby in that pram they had mounted onto skis and often hitched up to the family Ski-Doo. It was at the handlebars of his snowmobile that he'd broken out into pimples, that at age fifteen he'd won his first professional race on the track at Brûlé, and it was naturally during an Ookpik rally a few years later that he met Mama, a young, fearless Amazon riding a vehicle as powerful as his own. She, too, had grown up on a snowmobile. Clinging to her father's back like a papoose, she had whizzed along the trails since her earliest days; and when she was five, she'd begun riding her first Ski-Doo at Christmas time, a miniature model that actually worked. Realizing that his life would no longer have any meaning unless it included this exciting Nordic Eve, my future father set about winning her. He pursued her ardently beneath the dense foliage. He courted her with an ambulance driver's sense of urgency, and my future mother responded favourably to the humming advances of this tall yeti with the appealing smile. It was on a snowmobile that they dated, got engaged, went to their wedding ceremony, then drove away at the head of a roaring torchlight procession. It was on a snowmobile again that they reached the isolated log cabin deep in the heart of the woods that was to house them during their honeymoon; and it was undoubtedly on the seat of their frisky snow scooter that I was conceived, in a great rustling of hurriedly unzipped nylon.

After the wedding, my parents decided to settle in the neighbouring town of Villeneuve, the North Shore's industrious heartbeat, where jobs were up for grabs. This is where I came into the world and reached the one-metre mark. But the old village of Ferland was only a half-hour's drive away, and we went back there every summer because of the sea and the lingering memory of the primordial amoeba. We returned to it even more often in winter, to enjoy the snow, since Ferland remained a snowmobiler's paradise; from the backyard, at my maternal grandfolks' place, you could get to the bush along the corridor created for Hydro-Québec's pylons, which spell their monotonous hinterland alphabet in giant letters all the way to Nunavik. Every winter weekend then, the ancestral residence at Ferland was a springboard for those wilderness fanatics my dear parents happened to be. But I often let them go off by themselves, for even though I'd inherited Papa's famous pram-on-skis and they had regularly carted me around in it, I was immune to the hereditary snowmobile virus. Not that I was allergic to the machine — I knew how to compete on occasions in a good race on the snow-covered beach and there were times when it exhilarated me to cleave through the dazzled darkness of a silent northern forest — but unlike my parents, I didn't make it a reason for living. I quickly had my fill of endless space and disapproved of any kind of racket made in the open air. I was against the premature thawing of tiny furry creatures, against terror being struck into the hearts of nice little squirrels. My personal world had loftier interests, and certain harmless vices, such as reading. To the pristine whiteness of snowy glades, I preferred the less immaculate but, in my eyes, so much more thrilling expanse of the pages of a book. And while my parents were having a ball in Siberia, I would much rather savour some horror story and piping-hot chocogrunts in Grandmother's bay-windowed living room. This is precisely what I had decided to do on that day, that calamitous Saturday in February when my world crumbled. In a way, one could say that reading saved my life.

* * *

It was the kind of day that jolts the mercury into a nose-dive. The stinging north wind howled like a banshee, and that was nothing compared to the blizzard being forecast for the evening, but it would have taken a lot more to intimidate my parents. Those stout-hearted children of Thule weren't about to give up their exciting weekly cross-country ride on account of such a little thing; it was all they'd been looking forward to the whole week. And after the motor of their Polaris started up without rebelling unduly, they had vanished into the blowing snow. They'd promised to be back at dusk, but the sun travelled across the sky and sank without waiting for them. Our supper congealed on our plates while we took turns at the window, watching out for them to emerge from the snowstorm that had just begun. Finally around eleven o'clock, headlights lit up the yard, but they were those of a police car, and two contrite constables turned up in our frantic living room to stun us with terrible news. A long way off in the darkness, fifty-four kilometers north of Ferland, the QTI train from Pineshish in the Monts de Fer stood still in the eye of the chaos with its two hundred cars of iron ore. And scattered all about the track were the remains of my father and those of his noble machine. They had found Mama an hour later. She had been ejected at the moment of impact and catapulted into a snowdrift well away from the rails. She was frozen when they put her onto the chopper. It wasn't until they got her to the hospital that they noticed she was still breathing. Her condition was considered critical: fractures, concussion, serious hypothermia. They didn't know if she would survive.

They couldn't quite figure out what had happened. The train had struck my parents while they innocently sped along the railway track. Most likely, they hadn't heard its horn because of their helmets and hadn't seen anything because of the blizzard. A lapse in concentration, carelessness, a miscalculation, and other stupid things. The kind of event that should never happen but happens anyway, just to hurt people. A statistical blip. Or rather blatant incompetence, in my opinion, on the part of the Guy in Charge of Special Effects. An illustration of his indifference or even his cruelty. Yoo-hoo, up there on your cloud! Did you enjoy yourself, you celestial psychopath? Did you snicker up your sleeve? But I'm talking nonsense. The cloud is sure to be unoccupied, and in the end God may be nothing more than a mothy myth.

It was only at the funeral parlour, in front of a closed coffin, that they dared to give me the last and worst detail. My heart was in shreds as I stood by the insidiously gleaming box that concealed my father's mortal remains, and I rebelled. I couldn't accept that I wasn't allowed to gaze at his face one last time. I demanded that they unscrew the lid. Grandfather led me to the adjoining room and explained why that was impossible: Papa's body had only been partially recovered. Among other anatomical gaps, his head was missing. It had been crushed by a hundred steel wheels. I remember feeling dizzy all of a sudden, and numb with cold although the radiators were boiling hot. The last thing I can recall before I toppled over and everything faded to black, is the quiet music. That blasted cantata gliding through a haze of incense. It was enough to make one loathe Bach for the rest of one's days.

Obviously, then, snowmobilitis was a sickness that could be fatal. I'd heard it said that passion was like that — it made people lose their heads. Now I had proof of it.

3

Mama at least isn't dead. She continues to live in spite of that nasty bash on her head from the train, but she lies slumbering in an Arctic more distant than the Pole. Beyond dreams even, say the medics. That's all they're able to say, though; Mama is outside the scope of their textbook knowledge.

Every day, we go and watch her sleep at the hospital in Villeneuve, and I linger by her bed for a long time, bent over her elfin face. Her brow, a virgin snowfield. Mama, Nelligan's frozen pond. On the screens around her, nothing happens. Mama blinks, Mama twitches, Mama breathes. But the EEG curve remains flat. She's asleep, moored to our world only by the tube that feeds her. Nothing but liquids, like a plant. Mama is one of those flowers that have been put away in a cupboard, plunged into an artificial winter. Here, at least, there is plenty of light. Her room is on the fourth floor, and through the window you can see the islands floating in the bay.

The doctors maintain that she can't hear anything, but we talk to her just the same. Grandmother chats with her and imagines her replies. As she sits there knitting tons of mittens, she fills her in on the village gossip while I brush her hair. And when Grandmother leaves the room to go and say hello

13

to her friend Armande in the long-term-care ward, I finally have a chance to look after Mama in my own way. I stretch out close to her and rub her cold limbs. She is like a soft statue. To warm her freezing hands better, I slip them underneath my thick sweater against my bare skin. I never cry; I'm too afraid she might hear and be upset. I save my tears for the nighttime.

They don't know when she'll come back to us, or if she'll ever emerge at all, but I have faith. I know she won't abandon me.

* * *

My grandfolks have prepared a bedroom for me upstairs and, to lessen the anxiety they exude concerning me, I do my best to smile. After Villeneuve, with its supermarkets, its traffic lights, and its port which attracts ore carriers from all over the world like a magnet, I felt funny ending up in Ferland. It's a place unlike any other, a kind of magical village where anything that happens keeps people's tongues wagging for a long time. The hamlet has a history that's more or less my own, since it was my fourth great-grandfather who hit upon the preposterous idea of founding it two hundred years ago. The one and only street bears my name, in fact; it stretches out over ten kilometres and links the three hundred houses that have shot up over the years between Pointe-Rouge and the Gigots. The Uapush River drenches the heart of the village and, at its mouth, set back a little on the headland, stands the red-and-white house where my mother grew up, which is now going to be mine for a while.

Ferland is the sea. On the map, it's still only the Gulf, but an exceptionally clear sky is needed for the bluish mirage of the South Shore to loom dimly into view. It's a crossroads where the elements meet, a natural crucible where the wind merges with the forest and the waves. Ferland swings between silence and howls, the dog-days and absolute zero; it's a land haunted by gods older than the Guy in Charge of Special Effects, a hideout of imaginary freebooters and woodland giants, a shuddering parable of the world's creation, an enclave where the storytellers are better than on TV. In winter, the bay is a cryogenic wilderness, a lunar landscape enlivened only by the occasional bold appearance of a federal icebreaker, but, in the end, spring always prevails, and in summer it's a transplanted bit of Scandinavia, a fawn-coloured sandy beach edged with ammophilous plants, a procession of tufted dunes. Ferland is a starry night, and when a gentle southern breeze caresses the sea so that it glitters like a dark jewel, Ferland is a living mirror, a rippling, eerie expanse of milky moonlight.

* * *

My grandfolks form an odd couple. *He* is kind of a

stiff beanpole next to whom even a scarecrow would look elegant, while *she*'s a bubbly little thing, always impeccably turned out. The son of a real post-office employee of Her Remote Majesty — complete with sleigh, dogs, and big frosty beard — Grandfather served the queen himself when he was young; he was the village telegrapher. He still takes care of the local mail in an office adjoining the house, and in his spare time he smokes a legendary salmon — sweet, aromatic flesh that melts in your mouth as though it were the pulp of an exotic fruit. Grandfather enjoys telling scary tales. In the evening, when we make a fire on the shore, he crams my head full of the most dreadful lies and other fabricated true stories in which daring sailors and fearless trappers challenge a whole pantheon of primitive deities. He'll take advantage of the occasion to uncap a few of the beers he hides in his salmon smokehouse. Because, by grandmotherly decree, all alcohol is forbidden in the house, owing to the overindulgence the old man is supposed to have been guilty of in earlier days. But he's much more temperate now; he sticks to three or four bottles of beer which he knocks back in an inconspicuous way.

Grandmother tends to be acerbic. With her husband, she's not very gentle, but on poor, darling little me she lavishes an inexhaustible amount of affection, and it feels good to snuggle up to her outdated perfume. Grandmother runs a tight ship at home. For her, hygiene is a cardinal virtue. When I come back from a swim in the summer, she forbids me to step inside until, on the look-out for some treacherous grain of sand, she has inspected even the spaces between my toes, and Grandfather himself is often forced to take off his clothes on the verandah when he returns from the smokehouse. Grandmother is proud, and concerned about her appearance. She keeps track of all the new fashion trends, and her husband's sloppy dress upsets her. What a disgrace for her to have to be seen in public on the arm of that caveman! She would love to take him shopping in Villeneuve, but that's a pipe dream because the mere sight of a shopping mall makes Grandfather break out into a cold sweat.

She knows he is storing bottles in his lair. At least she has the satisfaction of having purged the house of them. She would like to root out his cigarette smoking, too, but since he's adamant on that point, she shifts the battle onto the psychological level: with the foil from his empty packages, she is making a lead ball which gets bigger from year to year, symbolizing the relentless progression of the cancer that will carry him off some day. Grandfather refuses to let this frighten him; he lights up as soon as she produces her ball, and he accuses her of mental cruelty. She retaliates by rebuking him for his recklessness. In return, he reproaches her for bossing him around, to which she replies that he's nothing but a stubborn old caribou. Clashes of this kind happen often, and things can get ugly. Lacking her gift of the gab, Grandfather is always the first to run out of verbal ammunition. From then on, he only answers in Morse, an idiom she doesn't know, which allows the old man to express himself with a crudeness that would otherwise be unacceptable. I happen to know the code, and this puts me in the difficult position of being the interpreter. I do my best to come up with euphemisms. I'm the UN peacekeeper; I try to prevent the situation from getting out of hand, but my ability to intervene is laughable, and their squabbles often turn into wholesale massacres. She will call him a drunkard, he calls her a bingo addict. She condemns his grubbiness, he berates her meagre charms. Thus, they climb the smooth rungs of the deliberate-insult ladder until they reach the high plateau of the supreme outrage: she blurts out that he is senile; he retorts that she's nothing but a nosy old snoop. No allegation in the world could possibly affect either party more deeply. Which doesn't mean they aren't justified. It's true that Grandfather is subject to crazy ideas that can only be explained by his advanced age. He *does* occasionally see German submarines slip by offshore and reports them to the coast guards who politely promise to look into the matter. It's no less a fact that Grandmother, under cover of darkness, often tiptoes down into the post-office to steam open certain letters from women in our neighbourhood. But when they arrive at this level of viciousness in the expression of the truth, all contact is broken off. Grandfather slams the door and heads for the smokehouse to get sloshed, while Grandmother starts sewing furiously, swearing that she'd rather cut her own throat than speak to him again.

But they're never able to remain angry for long. The following day, Grandfather comes knocking on the door and offers his apologies, as well as a bouquet of flowers. Grandmother accepts the flowers but never the apologies, and invites him instead to sit down to eat one of his favourite dishes. On those evenings, I go up to bed early so as to leave them alone for a bit and, at night, through the partition wall, I can hear their bed creaking. I know that soon the recriminations will start pouring out again, but for now they've called a truce. For a little while, a few days perhaps, they will love each other, craziness and all, and verses from the Song of Solomon will be murmured in quiet corners of the house.

* * *

Apparently, my school year is in serious jeopardy. My grandfolks want to enrol me in the village school. I have nothing against that. Actually, I couldn't care less; I'm too busy dwelling on my unhappiness to be interested in such trivialities. I am stewing in a sombre juice. I try to be strong, but this darkest hour of my fractured existence seems to go on for ever. I have lost interest in the job of living. All I'd like to do is sleep and rest in peace myself, but even that is denied me, because I am constantly attacked by horrible night terrors.

I dream about that spot, fifty-four kilometres north of here. In my nightmares it is a shifting maze with walls of nocturnal gusts of wind. It's a labyrinth whose floor is spanned by glittering rails, where I wander about, frozen like a rat, searching for the exit. Worst of all is that thing I hear prowling around nearby corridors. That Jurassic creature tooting its horn, and searching, too. I move forward, because that's better, but I die at the thought of meeting its stare. I run away, trying to burst out of the dream, and at long last I'm propelled into the anguish of my bed, thinking I still hear the monster roar beneath my window and feeling the whole house shake at its approach. Then there's only my bed, and finally just me.

It's like that every night. My dreams are sick. The only remedy is outwitting sleep. Rather than facing the Minotaur of Kilometre 54, I take refuge in my books and break all reading records. I'm a voluntary insomniac and often emerge as the winner of this endurance test that pits me against the night. The first glimmer of dawn is my reward, daybreak my ephemeral trophy.

4

In the hope of saving whatever formal education I have left, my grandfolks finally sent me to school. I don't see any point to it since May is almost over, but I've agreed to go just to please them. They probably want to get me out of the house, make me see people my own age, take my mind off things. Let's reassure them: let's act as if things were getting back to normal.

* * *

There was only one unoccupied desk in the sixth grade, at the very back, with a radiator and view of the sea, next to Luc Bezeau. That's how we ended up being neighbours, cousins almost, by force of institutional spatial realities. This kinship, mind you, is simply a figure of speech, because Luc has reacted to my arrival with utter indifference. I accept this fate and resign myself to gazing all day long at his 'what planet is this?' profile. He just doesn't look with-it. That prow-like face, pierced by hypnotic gimlet eyes. He's definitely out of place among the rosy young Vikings, crammed with vitamins, who fill the school. On top of this, there's the aroma of forgotten cod that hovers about him at all times. I hope he won't suddenly decide to take off his boots...

* * *

In his own way, Luc is a model student. He always maintains an Olympian calm; he's the champion of silence. Never, ever, does he goof off or create an uproar. Actually, he never opens his mouth, and the teacher is careful not to question him, as though she knew he wouldn't answer anyway. Between the two of them, some kind of cause-and-effect relationship is at work, but the other way around. Luc doesn't try to find excuses, he lives inside his bubble without bothering anyone. Glued to his desk, completely still, he looks out of the window at the sea for long stretches of time or stares down at his eraser as though he were doing his best to make it levitate. The rest of the day, he draws — he's a talented sketcher. His margins are full of skilfully rendered fish and lizards. Sometimes he also jots down a few lines of poetry in a peculiar alphabet he has perhaps dreamt up himself. It's unreadable but it must mean something, because you should see him labouring away with his tongue sticking out as he polishes his useless haiku! No doubt about it — an active mind lurks beneath that weird shell. In any case, he's smart, because even though he often misses school, his marks are among the best. He reads a lot: he chooses huge tomes at the library, science books ahead of the curriculum, mainly stuff on marine biology.

* * *

I've given up trying to cross the canyon of mistrust that separates our desks, but my eyes keep being drawn to him. I can't help it; I study his clown-like noggin with an entomological interest and wonder what thoughts might be fermenting in such a receptacle. But Luc remains as indecipherable as his poems. His eyes avoid meeting mine. He erases me from his field of vision. I should do the same and concern myself with what's happening on the blackboard instead, but his stubborn denial of my existence is beginning to look like a provocation, a challenge I have to meet — it's a question of pride, of asserting myself, of taking my revenge by laying siege to him. It's comforting to know that his coldness isn't just directed towards me. The distance he puts between us isn't more galactic than the one he keeps between himself and all of mankind. Luc behaves as if nothing or no one had any importance, as if he were the only real inhabitant of a virtual universe. During recess he stands apart and traces arabesques and mystical circles in the gravel with his toe. I think it's some kind of illness — a mental one or something to do with Molière — which is called misanthropy. I don't know if it's genetic, or because

23

he might have been rejected at the very beginning, or if Luc has actually chosen to exclude himself from Ferland's young people, but, whatever the reason, he's certainly the most unpopular guy in our school. Nobody would dream of inviting him to their birthday party, and he wouldn't go anyway. A voluntary castaway, a singlehanded sailor, that's what he is.

* * *

The Cyclopes *do* seek Luc's company, but of all the unwelcome associations, this is definitely the one he could most easily do without. The Cyclopes are a gang of deranged louts who are into gas fumes and heavy metal. Their leader is Réjean Canuel, a huge rocker whose duds swarm with skulls and swastikas and who's repeating sixth grade. He boasts about having a real uncle doing time in the Port-Cartier penitentiary. The boss takes a sadistic delight in hounding the young crowd on the beaches, but Luc is the beneficiary of his special attention. He has nicknamed him 'the Mongolian' because of his oriental gaze and has made him his official fall guy, the one you kick around, the one you taunt. Not a day goes by without Luc having got a taste of it: they toss his cap into the can, they stuff old fish into his locker, they dump the contents of his schoolbag into a garbage pail. Legends circulate about his Cyclopean misadventures: mention is made of a certain bottle of laxative they're supposed to have forced him to swallow, and also of an entire day he is said to have spent shut up inside the school's trash container. It's reported that Canuel's favourite sport involves taking off Luc's clothes in the winter and chasing him all the way home. These rumours should obviously be taken with a grain of salt. Yet the mere sight of the Aryan enthusiasm with which Luc is being harassed is enough to give the most unlikely stories an aura of plausibility.

He puts up with all this as if it were quite normal. His strategy is to not react. Never, ever, does he run away or make the mistake of defending himself. You never see him complaining or begging them to stop. After they've tripped him up, he simply gets back onto his feet and continues on his way. If they shove him into a garbage bin, he waits for his tormentors' hilarity to subside, then extricates himself calmly from the refuse. When they pound him a bit too hard, his eyes flash and his fists clench, but the fire never spreads, the explosion never takes place. His stoicism is remarkable but has the serious disadvantage of irritating Canuel and stimulating his viciousness. In the peaceful but stubborn resistance Luc puts up against him, the young cock-of-the-walk thinks he detects an element of arrogance, and he may be right. In any event, he has vowed he'll make his fall guy break down before the school year ends. To see Luc cringe, to hear him moan — that's the wish he's trumpeting about. He has made this a point of honour, and it seems unlikely that Luc will be able to hold out for very long. Yet nobody considers intervening. This is understandable, really: who would want to risk his neck for a dirty dog like him? Bystanders prefer simply to get used to the sight of him being tortured. They pretend they're witnessing an experiment designed to establish the humiliation tolerance limits in the common Mongolian.

I wouldn't want to be in his shabby boots. To think I used to believe I had the monopoly on bad luck! Until now, I just couldn't imagine anyone having been born under a more ominous star than my own, yet it is so; Luc is the temporarily living proof of it. I wish I knew how to put an end to the odious corrida, but I'm exactly like the others — chicken, fearful, too worried about my own survival. Since I don't have the guts to do something, I simply observe all this as though it were a conflict in some foreign country, while deep down feeling vaguely ashamed. I keep telling myself that in every school in the world the life of scapegoats such as Luc is governed by a natural law he has no choice but to submit to, like the rest of us.

5

As the school year draws to a close, doubt takes root
in the minds of those who have bet on the Cyclopes,
for even though the full force of his evil genius has
been brought into play, Canuel is unable to break the
Mongolian. Day after day, Luc resists like a bullet-
proof robot. I have no idea how he does it. Could it
be related to his father, who is crazy, so they say, and
who supposedly puts him through the mill? Does he
train at home perhaps? The fact is that he takes it
all, endures treatment that should have turned him
into a quivering jellyfish a long time ago. In his own
way, he's admirable. Seeing him standing there while
bombs rain down on him, with a flimsy umbrella
of patience as his only defence, is a beautiful sight.
It teaches us all a good lesson. The example of his
courage pushes me to probe my inner self in search
of a similar resource and awakens a dim yearning
— a desire for power, a taste for action, a wish to be
just as strong and invincible as he is. Strange, isn't
it? Who would have thought the Mongolian could
become a source of inspiration?

* * *

I don't know what finally drove me to intervene. The

27

need to pay Luc back a moral debt because he is making me feel stronger? A wave of pity? A sudden itch to do something heroic? A death wish? Perhaps all these things were intermingling in the unconscious regions of my personal geology, simmering away in my interior magma, that brew of volatile urges so ready to erupt. In any case, I stepped forward to come to Luc's defence.

Yet it was a beautiful Saturday in June, not a suspicious-looking cloud in the sky, one of the first truly euphoric days of summer. I was just coming out of Langlois's convenience store with a goodly supply of humbugs, thinking only about my imminent glucose orgy, when I spotted Luc and the jeering Cyclopes who were surrounding him. They'd waylaid him as he came back up from the beaches with the bounty from a fruitful hunting expedition: two big bags filled with precious bottles. The one-eyed monsters intended to impose a tax on the Mongolian's load, and since he didn't have the basic good sense to agree with them, they'd undertaken to murder him at a leisurely pace, beginning with the extremities and paying particular attention to the soft parts. Honestly, I don't know what came over me, but when I saw all of them go at poor Luc at the same time to tear him apart, I was actually weak enough, impulsive enough, to advance towards them to protest. I didn't realize until after the fact just how foolish that was.

Already, I regretted my move, but it was impossible to undo: I was caught in the eye of the Cyclops. An astonished stare at first at such audacity, but the novelty seemed to appeal to Canuel, who was no doubt already assessing my fall-guy potential. As for Luc, that commodity about to be rendered unusable, he looked clueless, totally zonked out. Since no one ever stood up for him, he didn't know how to react, I suppose. Meanwhile, Canuel had gone beyond the pensive stage and, flashing his famous shark-like grin, he swaggered quickly towards me. I tried to back away, but one of his cronies, a big idiot melodiously called Bacaisse, tripped me up, so that, already defeated and repentant, I toppled over like a tree in Témiscamingue. The king of the cannibals leaned over me. He looked famished enough to swallow me hook, line, and sinker, and I clenched my teeth, waiting for the pain to begin. But just when my windshield was about to be shattered, an amazing thing took place. Luc, that human punching bag, that advocate for nonviolence, our local Gandhi, all of a sudden turned into a ferocious creature. Struggling like a wildcat on a hot stove, he somehow got away from the muscleman who restrained him, launched himself at my predator, knocked him over, and held him down on the ground. The apes howled, then there was a collective but brief rush towards the fighting pair, abruptly cut short by the sight of a knife that had materialized out of nowhere and was being held at Canuel's throat by Luc. The young Nazi was pale as a ghost. He kept desperately swallowing his Adam's apple. Was he going to be treated to the tracheotomy of his dreams? He peed in his jeans, but no one laughed because we were all on the point of doing the same thing. Luc pressed down on the blade and I thought this was it, that he yielded to the temptation to give the brute a second life as a loaf of Wonder Bread. But, in the end, he merely spoke, uttering these weighty words in the terrified lout's face:

'Your bones are going to turn white in the tropical sun.'

It slid out of his mouth like a felt bootie over a waxed floor. And it struck me that this happened to be the first time I heard Luc speak, but what surprised me wasn't so much what he said, but the sonority of his voice, which sounded solemn, amazingly mature. I'm sure Canuel was flummoxed by that tropical bit, but he took the cryptic allusion to his bones seriously and shrank back even more. Luc stood up and walked away from the invertebrate while keeping the other cretins, stunned by the unfamiliar sight of a fearsome Mongolian, at a respectful distance. Canuel hauled himself back onto his feet with difficulty. He felt his throat and tried to bark something out, no doubt an order for a massive attack, but the only sound he managed to produce was a squeak resembling that of an asthmatic mouse. Picking up the tatters of his smashed authority, he pointed a vindictive index finger at us. Then he turned on his heels, which were accompanied by the rest of him as he staggered away, followed by his bewildered werewolves.

We had conquered the Cyclopes. I was too flabbergasted to rejoice, and Luc wasn't exactly in a triumphant mood either. As soon as the defeated bullies had disappeared, he put his knife away in his boot and proceeded to inspect his bottles, assessing the damage. Reassured at last about the condition of his glass treasures, he turned towards me. I expected a word of thanks or something like that, at the very least some sign that we were in this together, but all I got was a sidelong, reptilian glance, as if he blamed me for sticking an unwelcome nose into his business, thereby forcing him to reveal the fiery secret of his innermost nature. He picked up his bags and stepped into the convenience store, leaving me standing there as if I were the last, irrelevant pin left in a tedious bowling game. Anger surged through me. I couldn't get over it. I thundered all the way home, cursing the Mongolian's immeasurable arrogance, but railing especially against myself and my stupid humanitarian move.

The nerve of him to go on ignoring me! Didn't I stick out my neck so far for him it almost got snapped off? Does he think incurring the wrath of the Cyclopes is no big deal then?

* * *

The night glowed red with bloody premonitions. Hour after hour, my anxious mind conjured up the various forms — each one more harrowing than the next — Canuel's retaliation might take. I saw his telescopic stare homing in on me. I pictured horrifying surgery sessions without benefit of anaesthetic and blasted Luc for being so hideously ungrateful. But daybreak shed a different light on his apparent callousness. When I went out onto the verandah, I found on the bottom step an object he'd obviously left there specially for me: an engraved seashell with a painted lizard on it just like the ones he sketches on everything. It's a pretty little thing, precious no doubt in the mind of its creator, and when I held it up to the first rays of dawn for a better look, I understood it was a present, a token of his gratitude.

6

Luc doesn't waste words. He belongs to that breed of taciturn zebus that make good monks and rodeo champions. He's a kind of insulated dreamer, but after a while you get used to his clam-like ways as well as that solitary-confinement mug of his, and you even begin to find him amusing. The two of us have performed 'the crab,' clutched claws to seal a pact. More than anything else, it's an alliance against the Cyclopes, because those horrible brutes are still on the prowl. We come across their troll tracks here and there, but so far they haven't attacked. Could it be that Canuel is afraid of crossing swords for the second time with Zorro of the Beaches? Has he perhaps dropped our duo of disagreeably bristly hedgehogs from his menu? It could also just be a strategy to get us to let down our guard — perhaps all he's waiting for is an opportunity to squeeze us into individual packets. Not being mind readers, we prefer to see ourselves as the ingredients of a potential recipe and not take any chances. We only travel as a team now and spend our days behind a martial façade. To deter the enemy, we've stockpiled a quantity of slings and clubs made out of bits and pieces of two-by-fours. To Luc's trusty knife, I've added the baby machete my uncle Hugues sent me from Africa for

Christmas. Even though all is quiet on the war front in this month of June, we do our best to look wide-awake and mean — indigestible.

The crab is a set of unspoken rules, a way of living together which we invent as we go along. Our partnership isn't limited to a joint defence; we now go bottle hunting together. And there's no better time for this than June, when the caplin wriggle all night long spellbound in the torches' glow. Every evening, a great snake of fire uncoils along the shore, and worshippers of the tiny fish hover around a hundred pyres. It's a plebeian crowd, made up of all the various categories of mankind: bowlers who've just wrapped up a tournament, carousing Knights of Columbus, Americans on vacation, mulish old hippies who wreck our fences as they try to rustle up more firewood, flabbergasted European tourists brandishing trout nets, and real fishermen too — boots up to their waists, armed with salebardes.

Luc and I prospect for business. Sauntering from one tribe of merry gypsies to the next, we chat with anyone about anything, but particularly about miraculous catches, while out of the corner of our eye we check out the liquid supplies. Because these wondrous fishermen are unfailingly thirsty. They strew about the right kind of bottles, the returnable kind, the ones we can get good money for and, in anticipation of the following day, we note the locations of the more substantial lots, mapping out in our minds the long journey through the wilderness.

You have to know how to save your steps, since hunting means collecting scattered booty. It's a bit like trapping, only less cruel. Or more Icelandic: our bottles are like the eiderdown the local people gather there — fragile, difficult to ferret out, always richly deserved. Because beautiful as they may be, the beaches can be long. You need sturdy calves as well as guts, but you have the satisfaction of walking away with a full bag, the joys of free enterprise — and the profit, of course. At five cents a crack, it quickly adds up to a tidy little sum. Ambition overtakes us. We already want to expand, widen our market, increase the rate of production. We don't even wait for daybreak anymore to go hunting: last night we took advantage of the excitement generated by the first batches of caplin to slip into the tents of some plastered college students and swipe two cases of beer. We emptied them into the parched sand while taking the odd sip, proud to be doing such a booming business. This week I made twelve dollars. I blew it on candy. Luc is less childish — what doesn't go up in cigarette smoke, he saves. He stashes his loot in an old tyre buried at the foot of the Gigots, that granite outcrop bordering the bay to the west, not far from his place.

* * *

He lives in a dilapidated yellow trailer that badly needs a new paint job. Plonked down in the middle of a bald yard, the shack is surrounded by lobster pots, punctured buoys, and car skeletons, but the shabbiness of the setting is redeemed by a magnificent, unbroken view of the sea. I haven't seen his mother, but his father owns a red truck that's being eaten away by rust and actually looks quite a bit like him — he's a big, dishevelled, red-haired guy, kind of a former sumo wrestler who wears revolting undershirts and seems as decayed as his vehicle. Physically, he and Luc appear to have nothing in common, other than the cap-wearing gene, but it's difficult to make a proper comparison because of the distance. For we always give Luc's place a wide berth and, whether his father is in evidence or not, he'll quickly drag me off in another direction.

Old Bezeau is a fisherman. That's how he earns his living and Luc often goes out with him. Through my binoculars I can see them riding the swells in their large boat. They croon to the cod for hours on end, haul in the occasional halibut, or follow a school of mackerel, and with their strong sea-fishing rods they'll pull in a full load of these silvery streaks. When they get back home, it's Luc who handles the job of cleaning the catch and arranging the portion that's going to be sold in a refrigerated container at the back of the truck. You should see him cutting up a fish! He does it the way he serves mass — the same efficiency, the same depth of concentration. Keeping out of sight at the crest of a dune, I watch him slice his herrings with expert precision and I realize just how close Canuel came to ending up on a fish-and-chips platter. Luc is a true master of the knife. With the flick of a wrist, he will slit a fish's belly, then smoothly scoop out the guts in one handful and fling them gracefully to squadrons of frenzied gulls. But first of all, he takes care of the head... All those heads he lops off, which tumble into the steel garbage can as from a tireless guillotine. I can't help adding, multiplying. This instinctive bit of mental arithmetic is actually a helpful dodge; it stops me from brooding over that other head, the one that is missing from the casket. That detached way Luc goes about it, the unrelenting pace, that awful inertia of a locomotive's wheel. Seeing Luc in action means grasping how destiny works and knowing that everything boils down to a question of scale. Why should my father's fate have touched the heart of the Guy who Runs the Show, when even a village oddball like Luc can behead an entire population of lower creatures in just one hour?

Mesmerized, I watch him cut and cut like a king to the heart of a subject. And I feel a sudden urge to clamber down and seek the advice of that Jivaro who is such an ace at getting rid of huge stacks of heads without batting an eyelid. But I restrain myself because I know he would be embarrassed. That's what the crab means too: a pact to keep silent on certain things, a gentleman's agreement by which we undertake to avoid all sensitive or awkward topics. Unlike Luc's herrings, we aren't going to spill our guts. We will be tight-lipped and honourable, sphinx-like. He stays out of my private business and I don't want to meddle in his. Even though I'm tempted, I am not going to quiz him about his ambiguous relationship with Mona Daigneault, the widow who wears those sensational bikinis, whom he goes to see every Saturday to cut the lawn or repaint bits of her fence. In the same way, the crab forbids me to question him about his intriguing solo hikes into the Gigots. These swallow him up for hours on end. At the risk of busting my face, I once tried to follow him into that maze of rocks and aggressive bushes, but the mountains have trails only *he* knows about, and soon, useless scout that I am, I lost my way. I had to backtrack without having the slightest clue what he might be doing up there, and we never talk about it since that's taboo. Luc is like those Russian dolls, one secret fits into another. He's a gumball — soft at the centre, I'm sure, but with a thick shell that takes you forever to suck. You have to accept him like this, with his cloaks, his closed doors, his dark hidden dungeons.

* * *

Luc likes to break the rhythm of the hunt's repetitive phrase. He inserts parentheses. This morning we swam all the way to the *Tila Maru*, a stranded ore carrier adorning the shallows at Pointe-Rouge, and explored the sharp-edged bowels of that rusted hulk. Yesterday, we outwitted the slack vigilance of a Gothic watchman and sneaked into the Silent Domain, where our macaw-like shrieks shattered the expensive peace and quiet of people who had come from afar to get away from it all. Each day there is a new adventure, another wacky plan: we'll parachute water-beetle commandos into the tadpole populations of Jules's marsh and cause epic battles in the hollows, we'll scour the spinal stretches of the Cap-aux-Os for dinosaur tracks, then go and listen to the lunar song of that haunted fault at the base of the Gigots into which a little girl is said to have fallen many years ago. Fed by these novel images Luc lifts from the warp and weft of an unfamiliar story, a new, fabulous, multidimensional vision of the beaches begins to form in my mind. I follow close on his heels and pretend I am a German tourist. I let him be my guide. I can tell he's trying to open a door to his soul for me. Being the sort of lock-jawed tridacna clam that he is, Luc explains himself better without words, by showing me through his private universe. It's his way of communicating, of tightening up our moorings and consolidating our alliance.

While scanning the beaches together, we discover their numerous peculiarities, but observe, as well, certain undocumented species of the local fauna.

There's the mysterious Madame Fequet. Her nubby curtains open only in the evening, when she sends coded signals to a furtive crabber who delivers cases to her by rowboat. There's Monsieur Groulx. He goes and sits down at the end of the old jetty every day to eat his orange and wait for a fiancée who told him she would meet him there eons ago but never showed up. There's Arthur, the door collector, who's always drilling holes in the walls of his big place so he can add yet another entrance, slowly transforming his home into a dangerous Gruyère. And then there's Father Loiselle, who stuffs his face all day long in the kitchen of the presbytery. As well as his spectacular bulimia, he has another claim to being special: he is Luc's friend. We often stop by to say hello, a courteous gesture we turn to our advantage by gorging on doughnuts and winkles. The priest has a serious circumference problem, but he says it's not his fault: it's because of the deplorable rivalry pitting all the cooks in the realm against one another — that conspiracy of the knife-and-fork, that plot to damn him by the sin of good living! Buried beneath meat pies and game pies, bombarded with buttery salmon and porpoise stews, crushed by blackberry tarts, French fritters, and fried bacon strips, the poor servant of the Guy who Runs the Show capitulated a long time ago, knowing he is doomed to the digestive torments of Hell. This doesn't stop Luc from holding him in high esteem. Loiselle is a man of great wisdom in his eyes; his respect for him is galactic. The good priest shows concern for Luc's welfare. He always inquires after his health and wants to know, too, how things are going at home — an issue he seems to feel some anxiety about. Luc's father is never mentioned in so many words, but I can guess he looms large at the heart of this uneasiness. One senses there is friction between the ecclesiastic and the fisherman, and Luc has revealed to me this is because of his altar-boy job. His father detests religion in general and Loiselle in particular. It drives him wild that Luc has gone over to the enemy and he demands an end to it, but Luc won't give in because he is fond of the priest. And so, in spite of paternal opposition, he continues to don his skimpy white vestment every Sunday and vows he'll keep it up, out of loyalty, if nothing else, to the first person ever to call him his son through the grille of the confessional-box.

* * *

Mama is Nelligan's frosty garden, that ice-sheathed pond lying north of any Norway, and there is no sign of an imminent thaw. I find comfort in the thought that I'm not alone in this ordeal, since Luc has a mother who has shipped out, too. She left soon after he was born. Disappeared, leaving only a name: Chantal Bouchard. Does Luc blame her, I wonder, for having abandoned him? He doesn't seem to, but he must miss her a lot, because he tries hard to remember her, conjuring up all kinds of different faces. In an exercise book, he collects mothers. In it, he has pictures he's cut out of magazines and catalogues, collages of photos in which he's hybridized Snow White and Vampirella, and combined the Virgin Mary with old *Playboy* centrefolds. It must be tempting to create an ideal mother for yourself, and Luc isn't exactly holding back. Perhaps he imagines himself, just for fun, living first with one, then with another, dipping as he pleases into that maternal harem. His *mother* book contains drawings as well; they are portraits, all showing the same sad, lovely face of a young woman with her hair streaming in the wind. When we visit Father Loiselle, Luc gets out his latest sketches and asks for his opinion, because at the time of Luc's christening the priest slightly knew the vanished Chantal and he agrees to guide Luc's pencil with whatever recollection he still has. Were her eyes like this? No, more like that. What about the curve of her eyelids? And what shape were her lips? Father Loiselle answers as best he can, and afterwards, taking advantage of a break during the hunt, Luc will bend over his exercise book to touch up that same portrait yet again, to try to improve it by proxy. Sometimes a feeling of helplessness overwhelms him and he tears up the page. Other times, when he's in a cubist mood, he will draw a strange

42

surrealist mother, half woman half fish, and then her hair will float among the waves. Anyhow, it's still a dreary game; Luc knows very well that paper mothers, even hundreds of them, can never equal a real one, whether she has shut up shop, as has mine, or not.

7

Even though we bagged precious little today, it was a big day for Luc because he tasted his first chocogrunts. I knew Grandmother had baked some before she headed out to a meeting of her sand-golf club, and I'd planned the attack. Taking advantage of Grandfather being busy, we stole into the house like smoke-shrouded djinn and drifted with spellbound nostrils all the way to the kitchen, where the tasty delights sat waiting for us. They were cooling on the counter — plump, enticing, *so* irresistible that we wolfed them all down before slinking off around the back. But I wasn't going to get off lightly. What a sermon at suppertime! Grandmother was appalled to have come home to a kitchen swarming with crumbs. To top it off, as if the culinary crime weren't heinous enough in itself, she had seen me slip out with Luc. She was utterly perplexed. With so many children from good, decent families living in our neighbourhood, she just couldn't understand why I'd chosen to team up with the 'Bezeau boy,' that filthy ragamuffin, that living violation of all the rules of hygiene and propriety. We argued loudly. Fortunately, Grandfather happened to be on my side and finally, after much quibbling, Grandmother acknowledged that perhaps Luc wasn't quite the pariah she had made him out to be. She admitted he couldn't be blamed for what he was, since, after all, he hadn't picked his father, and his altar-boy position might constitute proof of certain moral standards. She didn't forbid me to see him again, but I had to make a whole string of promises, such as never to set foot in his place, and to take exceptional precautions because of the possibility of contamination.

Poor Grandmother. I'm not surprised Luc baffles her. And to think that she's only judging him by his appearance, she doesn't even have a clue about his *real* eccentricities. Panic would strike at her heart if she saw us smoking away like a pair of old sailors and practising knife-throwing on that dummy pieced together from old buoys, which Luc has nicknamed Canuel. Or if she knew about our daredevil games and all those crazy acrobatic feats we indulge in among the steep crags at Pointe-Rouge. In Grandmother's eyes, Luc is a cactus, a censored version of the ugly duckling, without the swan at the end. She's unable to see beyond his exterior, but can you really blame her? To discover Luc's graceful side, you need to go for a long hike with him and watch him saunter along, free as the breeze. To understand his particular beauty, you have to throw him into the water and see him swim with the voluptuous exuberance of a seal. The gangly limbs and spatula-shaped feet that on dry land give him a penguin-like waddle, turn into natural flippers then and allow him to cleave confidently through the waves. Even his skin seems to grow supple under the briny caress of the gentle sea. Luc dives as joyfully as a porpoise and possesses a phenomenal amount of wind. If he wanted to compete in the apnoea tournaments held in July at the mouth of the river, no one would have a hope of beating him — certainly not I, since timing myself in the bathtub is as far as I've progressed.

The ocean courses through Luc's veins, and when he stops to gaze at it, you would think he was peering into himself. Entranced, he will kneel down at the water's edge and forget about everything else. From his throat will rise a series of fluty clucks, tongue-clickings, yelps like those of a sea lion. While he converses with the ocean in this way, don't try to speak to him; he won't even know you exist. He seems to be privately celebrating some primitive, elemental mass.

Anything to do with the Gulf's living organisms attracts his attention. Thanks to the books he reads, he can differentiate just as easily between species of fish and birds as between the various types of molluscs or algae. He is training himself, in fact, to classify them. The biological tree's complexity doesn't scare him; like a clever monkey, he leaps confidently from branch to branch in that mangrove swamp of phyla, suborders, and genera. He rarely needs to refer to the littoral-fauna guidebook he carts around in his satchel. Often, just for the fun of it, he'll ask me to open the book and pick any family of crustaceans or echinoderms, of which he then proceeds to reel off the various members down to the last subspecies, and he'll transform this gobbledygook into a marching song, some kind of rap in time with our footsteps. *Mesodesma arctatum — siliqua — costata — ascophyllium nodosum — strongylo dröbachensis...*

* * *

I took advantage of them being at sea to slip over to their place. I know their lair is forbidden territory, but that sinister hovel drew me irresistibly, and since the door was unlocked...

The shabbiness of the abode hit me square in the face. The trailer is filthy, with sand everywhere and country music wailing away on the radio. The kitchen counter crawls with dirty dishes. Fishing tackle lies about on the furniture among empty bottles and overflowing ashtrays. In the living room there are two sagging armchairs, a massive old Spanish TV, a medieval VCR, and scattered all over the place are the parts of a half-dismantled outboard motor. The bathroom is a cesspool. The smell alone would be enough to shorten Grandmother's life. In comparison, Luc's bedroom looks quite tidy. The walls are covered with fish and photos of Cousteau. But his father's den is filled with breasts and prehistoric odours. As I headed back towards the bay window in the living-room, I trained my binoculars on the open sea to make sure they were still fishing. They were definitely there, at the end of the lens — mites tossing and pitching on a Smurf skin. While I watched them, a glitter caught my eye. It flashed through my mind that they must have binoculars as well, that they could spot me, so I made a lightning-quick exit.

Luc sees to it that his father's path and mine never cross, and that suits me just fine. I picture him as a kind of dragon, and everything I hear about him sharpens that image. When Luc talks about his father, he calls him 'the Pig' and one can tell very quickly that he'd rather not owe anything to his genes. As far as I know, the Pig fritters away his life in the taverns of Villeneuve. His words are hard, like the palms of his hands, and his gestures rough. Luc is confined to drudgery, which he performs without grumbling because one needs to eat after all and have a roof over one's head come January. The Pig beats him regularly and hard. Notified by the teacher, inspectors from the Children's Aid Society have come to our school to question him a couple of times, but were unable to press charges, since Luc refuses to testify. He has explained to me why, but I'm not quite sure I understand: he knows he could have his torturer put behind bars if only he agreed to talk, but that is exactly what he doesn't want. He's afraid he would be deported, placed in a foster home in Villeneuve. And the very thought of such an exile fills him with anguish because he needs the sea to live. He's convinced he wouldn't survive far away from it, he would suffer the same fate as a crab lost in the wilds of the Sahara. So he puts up with it. He is biding his time until he'll be old enough to settle his scores with the Pig. He's used to it, after all. He's able to take a lot of punishment; kicks and insults are nothing new to him. The only thing he can't tolerate is the Pig attacking the good name of the woman who has run away. And the animal knows it. He takes advantage of it. The filthy Pig does it on purpose...

* * *

Luc knows divers, real frogmen. They work at the port of Villeneuve but prefer to live in Ferland in a rented cottage. There are three of them: Joël, Marc, and Luigi — bearded, brawny, strapping fellows, haloed with a heroic aura. Luc thinks they have the most wonderful job in the world. He does their shopping at the convenience store. In return, they let him hang around their place in the evening and listen in while they evoke the splendours and perils of the deep, the friendly behaviour of minkes, the fear of being mistaken for a seal and gobbled up by a killer whale. On Saturdays, when they look after their diving suits, Luc bombards them with questions, for he is dying to find out how these work. He'd give anything to have a go, but they can't let him on account of the law. Luc has no intention of getting arrested because of such pranks, so he has decided to buy his own diving gear. That's why he has been squirrelling away his bottle money. The problem is that at the current price of a diving suit, it will take him forever to scrape together the necessary amount, and Luc wonders sometimes if it wouldn't be simpler to learn to inhale and exhale directly into the water, like a fish. He asks for my opinion and, worst of all, he seems serious. Why not? he insists. Isn't *Homo sapiens* descended from the great primordial water salamander if you put things in their proper perspective? And what are lungs, from a Darwinian point of view, if not highly developed gills? He keeps at it, wants to know what I think, but I'm careful not to encourage such nonsense. He will let it go in the end and start talking about something else as he continues to inflate his tyre and yearn for that blessed day when at long last he'll be able to afford the diving suit of his dreams. While waiting to be rich enough to imitate whales, he makes do with admiring them. Oh, how he envies them when he spots the noble herds travelling past in the open sea! If they approach the shore to hunt krill or frolic near the water's edge, he swims towards them and slides down into the iridescence to watch their huge but nimble bodies glide by and crease the aluminous surface with their backs. He never tires of listening to their song, their clicking sounds. He likes overhearing their chatter. He'd love to know what these perpetual wanderers talk about, and it puzzles me too: what *do* they go on about in their magnificent Morse?

* * *

The ocean has sharpened his senses. From the frothing of the waves, the smell of the wind, the behaviour of terns and countless other signs, Luc can forecast the weather. It's a gift from the wide open spaces and violet horizons, the result of all those nights spent out of doors in a ripped old sleeping bag. Because he loves the sea so much he even sleeps with it. Why should that surprise me? Doesn't an odd duck belong near the water?

He dreams his boyhood away at the bottom of a dune in front of his place. Only the rain can dislodge him, but even then he'd rather take shelter under the upturned boat than inside the house. He says you sleep better on the beach, dreams are more vivid, and even when you're awake, there are always things to see. He speaks of wild animals, porcupines, moose, and every now and then a wolf in need of salt, slipping out of the forest and trotting right up to the shore to lap up a bit of vintage Atlantic. He paints a picture of those submarine fields of light he sometimes sees moving against the current in the open sea and describes that funny guy, that crazy golfer who'll come down to the beach on pitch-black nights to practise his swing with phosphorescent balls. He tells me about the comets, the phases of the moon, northern lights, novae, meteors, and makes it all sound like a brilliant fireworks display. Luc knows a thing or two about the stars.

He has made a study of the night, that dark cavern with gem-studded walls. He is a great configurer of heavenly bodies. Choosing to remain ignorant about ordinary constellations, he has invented his own, each one inspired by the sea: the Anemone, the Dolphin, the Seahorse, the Ray, the Barracuda...

Night and day, he is in harmony with the ocean's moods. He is serene when it is poised between tides, tumultuous when there's a swell coming on; he bristles when gales rage, and I predict that in January, as soon as the ice appears, he will shrink back into the deepest recesses of his shell. Actually, he hates winter and finds it unfair to have to be subjected to its tyranny every year. His birth in such a high latitude is an error, he thinks, which he vows to correct some day. He has equatorial ambitions. He would like to live in the Galápagos and bask under a gentle sky. He fantasizes about mangroves, warm waters with crystalline depths, fish flashing riotous colours. On those shores, in the blazing tropical sun, his bones are going to turn white some day. He swears they will.

8

Luc has asked if he could come to the hospital with me. He would like to see my mother. I wasn't really surprised; for quite a while I'd felt him circling the topic like a shark on the prowl. Poor Luc. He conjures up the most fantastic images of motherhood but doesn't know a thing about it. He only has the vaguest of notions of what a mother is. He's dying to find out, that's why he's so interested in mine. The mother of a friend is already better than an anonymous ghost, and he quizzes me constantly, wanting to know all about those famous maternal virtues people praise so highly on TV and everywhere else.

As for the hospital, I've said yes. I didn't see any reason to refuse — provided, of course, we go there without Grandmother's knowledge, because she wouldn't understand and would be climbing the walls. We'll take the bus early tomorrow morning and she'll never know. Luc was over the moon. Couldn't have been more excited if I'd handed him a ticket to the Galápagos.

* * *

We presented ourselves at the hospital at eight o'clock. Luc caused some dismay among the staff on Mama's floor with that snooty-octopus look of his, but they did let us proceed to her room. Once we got there, Luc had a sudden attack of nerves. He didn't want to go in anymore. It was as if the threshold marked a magical boundary he didn't dare cross. Since that's how it was, I left him standing in the hallway and went in by myself to take care of my dear crystal mother as usual. Luc lingered outside. His carp-like stare loomed in the doorway. He seemed hypnotized by the northern loveliness of the sleeping beauty. My mother did look dazzling. The slanting morning sun bathed her in a golden glow and turned the room into a mausoleum out of some science-fiction movie. Even though held hostage by the fifty-fourth kilometre, even though nearly dead, she was still beautiful, and I felt as proud of that as if I'd had something to do with it.

Luc finally tiptoed in, totally awed. He watched me gently warming Mama's waxen hand. Then he decided to imitate me, lifting her other hand and transferring as many calories to it as possible. We kept this up for quite a while, like a pair of hot-water bottles, one on each side of her, warming my mother by heating up her extremities. It was one of those freaky moments you feel you have already lived through once before. Time had broken down, and Luc took advantage of it to sink into a worshipping trance, while I caught myself seeing a kind of unlikely brother in him.

When we needed to leave, it was simply impossible to drag him away from the bed. He hung on to it for dear life, enraptured by the sheer nearness of my mother. I reminded him that Grandmother's regular visiting time was fast approaching and she might show up any minute, but he wasn't listening. Bewitched, he gazed hungrily at Mama and wouldn't let go of her hand. I sensed he would have liked to be left alone with her and I almost went out, but then I changed my mind since that wasn't my plan after all. I wasn't going to grant him such a privilege; he might have taken advantage of it to nibble her like a crab and kiss her greedily, just to see if it produced the same effect as in fairy tales. There is a limit to my generosity where my mother is concerned and, to make him understand, I marked out the private property of her beloved brow with jealous kisses. This shook Luc up, and he agreed at last to follow me outside, but not without casting one final enamoured-toad glance at my slumbering mother.

A feeling of uneasiness stayed with us all the way to the bus and ensconced itself between us on the seat. We were silent on the journey home. I felt guilty and terribly selfish. I blamed myself for having so abruptly cut short the cardiological experience, no doubt a crucial one for Luc, of being at long last in contact with a real mother. He watched the islands drift past beyond the bus window. He still didn't say anything while I did my best to take an interest in the speeded-up film of spruce trees that was being shown on my side. I jumped when I felt his hand on my shoulder. He was looking at me even more gravely than usual, and suddenly, as if he had read my mind, he put into words what I really thought:

'We'll have to wake her up.'

The expression in his eyes was candid, free from any ulterior motive. He was offering me his help. And a huge wave of emotion surged through me. Wake her up, yes, before it was too late. Wake her up before the hydrochloric bitterness had eaten too deeply into the pipes and the plumbing gave way. Wake her up before the lava of hope congealed, while it was still warm, because without her the world would slowly grind to a halt, because otherwise you couldn't really call it living anymore. Wake her up? Absolutely! But how?

Luc's eyes were yo-yos. He was deep in thought. His brain had gone on the offensive, neurons were firing away, the cerebral artillery was fully deployed. For a moment, I honestly believed that a seed of genius was germinating in the sweltering hothouse of his skull and a new idea was about to be born, an original solution, but as we left Highway 138 to turn into the village road, he simply stated that he would pray for Mama's recovery. Big deal! A whole lot of good that would do. But he seemed as pleased as punch to have come up with it all by himself.

Later, in the evening, it occurred to me that it was

perhaps as good an idea as any. Possibly, I'd been wrong to condemn the Guy who Runs the Show so quickly. What do we really know about the pressures gods are under? Deciding to give the Über Space Surfer one last chance, I knelt down by my bed and offered him my apologies, begging him humbly to do something for Mama. I laid on the faith bit with a trowel because I wanted it to work, but after ten minutes I realized I was dialling into the void. There was no answer. It didn't even ring. The number was not in service. At least I knew where I stood: there is no puppeteer, no invisible strings. The Guy who Runs the Show is simply another Santa Claus you sooner or later just have to stop believing in.

It's tough to know you are alone. To make sure something more immense than my loneliness existed, I went over to the window and tried to measure the sea. Off to the west, Luc probably lay in his sleeping bag, busy smelling the stars, or praying perhaps. I hoped he would have more luck...

* * *

Usually Luc is waiting for me on the steps, but this morning he wasn't there. Luc late for a hunting expedition — that was a first, and I headed out to meet him. When I got to his place, I heard sounds, the tearful mumblings that serve as swearwords when he is angry. It came from beneath the upturned boat, and that's where I found him, prostrate and swollen. The Pig has thrashed him once again. I gathered the swine had sullied his mother, called her a slut, accused her of sleeping with every sailor in the port. I understood that he'd kept on trampling her like this until Luc couldn't take it anymore and reacted, giving the swine a perfect excuse for a thorough beating.

'It's all a pack of lies,' Luc said, jabbing the rowboat's ribs with his fists.

And through his sobs he defended his mother. She wasn't a tramp. Not at all. She was a virtuous woman. She had abandoned him, that was true, but he was convinced she must have had a very good reason, she must have had no choice. He just knew she was thinking of him wherever she might be. Some day she would come for him, he said, and the two of them would go away together, they'd go and live in the tropical sun. But, for now, there was only this breeze raking his hair, these glistening slugs coating his cheeks, that tentacular soreness burning all over. I tried to comfort him but didn't succeed. He wanted to be alone. He went off to the Gigots and I walked home, feeling sad. I wish I knew how to ease his sorrow. I wonder where that runaway mother is. Couldn't we try to find her?

* * *

This really is *too* odd for words. I couldn't get Luc's mother out of my mind and, since I felt in the mood to investigate, I went to see Grandfather in his smokehouse. While I helped him stir the brine, I questioned him about the mysterious Chantal and I could tell my queries bothered him, for he gave nothing but murky replies. He had hardly known Luc's mother, since she only lived in Ferland for a short time. A discreet young woman who didn't leave the house very often. Grandfather hadn't seen her anywhere but in church during the months before her death. Because she is dead.

She drowned in the bay one night in July, ten years ago, when Luc was just a baby. A swim that apparently ended in tragedy. Grandfather thinks she must have underestimated the currents and been swept along. In any case, her body was never found. Only her clothes, on the shore, the next day.

I seem to have been catapulted into the fourteenth dimension, and the landing is rough. What throws me is the way Luc talks about his mother, always in the present tense, as if she were alive. Yet he must know the truth. Or is it because he refuses to accept it? Does he believe she may have survived or swum away? At least that total fascination the ocean has for him makes more sense to me now. Those liquid arms he loves to melt into… Perhaps what he is looking for in those deep waters he so desperately wants to explore is a woman, his mother, who was swallowed up by the sombre sea.

9

Nitrogen narcosis manifests itself in hallucinatory phenomena and impulsive acts (removal of the mouthpiece, loss of a sense of direction, shedding of the mask, behaviour that is inconsistent or reveals a lack of concern for fellow divers, and so on), which may result in a diving accident (death by drowning, pulmonary overpressure, decompression accident...).

That business about Luc's mother really freaks me out, but I don't know how to bring it up with him. It's because of the crab, that anti-personnel crustacean who turns the terrain into a minefield, complicating the approach. Luc would have to be the one to broach the subject, but nothing indicates he has any intention of doing so. Very much the opposite, actually. He doesn't wish to talk about his mother's disappearance. He'd rather discuss how to wake up *my* mother, and that possible resurrection is fast becoming a major preoccupation for him. You don't need to be Freud to understand what is happening: Luc is transshipping into Mama's holds the cargo of attention he was never able to deliver to his own mother.

He has hunted up some medical encyclopedia

which he refers to constantly, reading up on anything related to comas, catalepsy, and tsetse flies.
He is familiarizing himself with the illness. We go to
see Mama nearly every morning, and Luc watches
what is going on, turns things over in his mind. He
observes the various medical procedures and disap-
proves totally. He is highly critical of the people who
are paid to treat Mama, to the point of questioning their competence. He doesn't think the medics
are going to get anywhere. He feels we should take
control. Since his prayers remain unanswered, he is
dreaming up other types of therapy, such as dragging
Mama out of bed and forcing her to walk. Not in
the least put off by my objections, he then tackles
the problem of warming my mother up and suggests
we wrap her in an electric blanket and turn up the
heating in the room as high as it will go. He comes
out with one crackpot idea after another, and I can
only forgive him for spewing such nonsense because
I know he means well.

Turning up the heat! Why not put her in a four-
hundred-and-fifty-degree oven while we're at it?
And how about a little electroshock on the side?

* * *

This morning, after we got back from Mass,
Grandmother gave me quite a surprise when she
told me she planned to invite Luc for supper. 'I'm
sure the poor boy doesn't often cook a proper meal.

It will do him good to eat a little,' she said almost
apologetically, as if to justify her sudden change of
heart. The Sunday display of Luc's skeletal structure
must have softened her at last. In any case, she asked
me to pass on the invitation. I fully expected Luc to
turn it down. I was convinced his natural shyness
would override any kind of stomach considerations,
but the day had another surprise in store for me:
he accepted on the spot. He promised to be here at
six. It's not until later that I realized how easily the
event could hit the skids. I know Grandmother; she
will take advantage of the opportunity to probe all
the recesses of Luc's mind, and I don't see how the
inborn wackiness that forms the very basis of his
character may be kept hidden. But it's too late to go
into reverse; what will be will be. I cheer myself up
with the thought that, as far as prestige is concerned,
Luc doesn't have an awful lot to lose.

* * *

He turned up on the stroke of six. He was in full
regalia, which included socks and a yellow shirt
that I took to be his formal attire. For her part,
Grandmother had worked like a dog on the grub:
the menu boasted scallop chowder, turbot with
olives, and a huge angel cake. There was enough to
feed an entire football team, and I was afraid Luc
might panic at the sight of such a gargantuan spread,
but fortunately he had understood the importance of

behaving in a civilized way. He came out of it with flying colours, calmly cleaning off his plate, gladly accepting a second helping, then a third, and battening it all down with half the cake. Grandmother was flattered, Grandfather full of admiration, and I was somewhat relieved. After serving the coffee, Grandmother went into gossip mode. Inquiring about Luc's academic results, she was delighted to hear they were among the top. Reassured about my friend's intellectual abilities, she asked him what he planned to do when he grew up. Luc declared he wanted to be a marine biologist. My grandfolks acknowledged that this was a worthy vocation and, if you stretched it a bit, perhaps even a useful one. Becoming more expansive as a result of the unanimous approval, he added that in any case, no matter what we did, the bones of every one of us would lie bleaching in the tropical sun one day. A block of ice smashing to pieces on the table would not have chilled the atmosphere more effectively. In an effort to save what was left of the furniture, I butted in with the explanation that Luc's macabre utterance should be taken simply as a philosophical statement about the futility of all human effort, or something like that, but I noticed how this only fanned the flames of Grandmother's distrust. Luc picked that particular moment to announce he was going to wash the dishes, and before anyone had a chance to react, he'd got down to work, gaily scalding the cutlery, juggling Grandmother's precious porcelain in the most terrifying way. I grabbed a tea towel and did my best to slow down the pace while the queen of the household hyperventilated at the end of the table and jumped at every bang, clink, or clatter.

A little later, while Grandmother inspected her dishes, looking for cracks, we — the men — stepped out onto the verandah to enjoy the breeze. Grandfather, who prides himself on being an astute weatherman, forecast an easterly wind at rising tide for the next day. Luc studied the skies, then agreed, but not without pointing out that there was a chance of a shower before noon, which made the old man shake with laughter. Since Luc is normally infallible in this domain, I have a feeling Grandfather won't be laughing quite so hard tomorrow morning as the rain beats down on the roof of the smokehouse, but he can always save face by citing beginner's luck. Meanwhile, the evening was balmy, a playful wind capered about, and suddenly the idea popped into my head of inviting Luc to stay overnight. At first, he thought I was putting him on. Then, when he saw I was serious, he accepted, as impressed as if I'd offered him accommodation at the Manoir Richelieu. Grandfather gave his consent, using teeth-clicking code. Grandmother seemed disturbed at the thought Luc would spend the night under our roof, but she didn't have the heart to turn me down, so she gave the go-ahead. Providing Luc's father approved, of course. My friend assured her that it would be perfectly all right with his dad, but Grandmother

64

insisted on getting his permission. She wanted to phone him, but Luc explained that their line had been cut off. He said he'd go and let his father know in person instead and jogged away along the beach. Half an hour later, after giving his legs a workout in the dunes, he showed up with the animal's hypothetical blessing. I didn't feel like reproaching him for this little white lie; I was only too happy it worked.

We lit a big fire and carbonized a full bag of innocent marshmallows. Then, when Grandmother went up to bed, Luc asked Grandfather to teach him teeth-clicking. The old man agreed to instruct him, and Luc turned out be an excellent pupil thanks to a solid jaw as well as a thirst for knowledge. After a single lesson he already knew the Morse code almost by heart and nibbled at the night like an old pro. Grandfather uncapped a beer and declared it was now storytelling time. We were treated to the tale of Jos Chibougamau, king of the Matagami lumberjacks, a zealous executioner of trees whom Grandfather claimed to have known personally in the days of his adventurous youth. A tribe of prickly boreal deities had decided to punish Jos by gouging out his eyes. Blinded, lost in the woods, he was overtaken by nightfall. As I stared into the flames, I could see him wander about while Grandfather's smoky voice hovered among the incandescent splutters. The tiny hairs on the back of my neck bristled when a vindictive tree toppled over on Jos, pinning him to the ground. And when legions of carnivorous beetles

65

gathered in a great crunching of chitin to crawl all over him and eat him alive, it seemed to me that the night itself leaned in to hear every word and shudder at the demented howls of the accursed lumberman. A hush greeted Jos Chibougamau's ghastly end. Then we threw ourselves at Grandfather's feet, begging him for another story. But he said no, because it was getting late. After urinating into the fire like giant firemen, we went up to bed.

There's another bed in my room and Grandmother had put clean sheets on it. We were too excited to sleep, but that was part of the plan. Actually, it was more or less for that reason I had invited Luc — so he could help me foil the ruses of sleep. He was thrilled by the many possible uses for teeth-clicking; he envisioned turning into a Morse teacher for cetaceans. After that, we talked about my mother's situation and how we might wake her up. Luc thought of administering a therapeutic shock: wishing to fight the train *with* the train, he suggested we play a recording of a tooting locomotive at top volume by her bed, but he did come around to admitting the idea was perhaps a bit far-fetched. Speaking of these things made me sad, and thinking about Mama brought tears to my eyes. When he saw me stranded at low tide, he did his best to refloat me, forbidding me to self-destruct in the next ten seconds and reminding me it was my duty to stay buoyant. He wouldn't let go. He kept maintaining there had to be a way to get Mama back, and that's when he asked me to tell him about my dreams. A foggy request — I didn't see the connection with my mother — but he explained how the solution to a problem nearly always came to him in a dream. He thought the key to Mama's wakening might be buried somewhere in my dreams, and he wanted us to analyse them together. The fog was clearing, but what could I possibly say about my dreams, since I had been dodging them for months now? I told him about my voluntary insomnia and the terrors that were the cause of it. For the first time, I gave a sparse description of Kilometre 54 with its labyrinthine torments, the horrifying pawing of the Minotaur, that iron monster. It did me good to talk about it and especially to see that Luc appeared interested. In his opinion, my refusal to sleep confirmed his theory — it actually explained my mother's endless swoon. This all seemed pretty obscure to me, but to him it was crystal-clear, and he returned to the charge with that business about dreams, urging me to stop fighting the night. He wanted me to sleep and, above all, dream, while remaining on the lookout for anything that might be related to my mother's resurrection. And thereupon he practised what he preached by passing out, abandoning me to my dread.

So here I am, writing by the faint glow of my flashlight, struggling through yet another pallid, bat-like night. I thought of following Luc's advice, but fear of Kilometre 54 wins out every time. I don't have the guts to dream, but that's not serious, since Luc dreams enough for both of us. He thrashes about in his sheets, gets all tangled up in them while uttering palatal sounds and fluty syllables. He is talking, no doubt about it. He is conversing with an unfathomable speaker in the liquid idiom of his poems. Will he mumble on like this until the gulls arrive?

10

Grandmother knew. She knew all about our trips to the hospital. She found out from a gabby nurse who couldn't keep his big mouth shut, but she wouldn't take action. I think it's because Luc shows such concern for her daughter's health. That touched her. Anyway, there's no more reason for us to be secretive: Grandmother has officially given Luc permission to come along. So we'll be going on our pilgrimages to Mama as a threesome from now on. That should simplify matters, if only from a logistic point of view.

* * *

I'm glad Luc joins us whenever we go to the hospital. The growing anxiety these visits generate is a burden we need to share among the three of us, since it's becoming more obvious every day that Mama is getting worse. She is wasting away. She is melting like a snow-woman in the heat of summer. The way things are going, I'll soon have nothing more to cherish than a bag of bones, yet the medics can't do anything. They're beaten. Left behind in the dust. Worthy representatives of the Guy in Charge of Special Effects, come to think of it.

Weighted down with my helplessness, I drag myself about. What can we do? What could we, poor ignorant boys, possibly try? How could we even dream of defeating the mighty physicians in charge of my mother on their home turf? I would happily sell my soul to see her re-open her eyes — if only some warm-hearted old devil turned up and offered to buy it.

* * *

Heaven-sent, coming to the rescue of the doctors, a blank-looking visiting specialist examined my mother and confirmed what we already knew: she is going downhill. He recommends that she be moved to a renowned experimental clinic in the capital where they deal with that kind of illness. But Quebec City is a long way away and I am dead set against it. I don't want them to ship Mama off to the ends of the earth, where she will be lost to us; the thought of her falling into the greedy clutches of a bunch of mad scientists turns my stomach. But Grandmother explained that we have reached the stage of desperate measures and may not have any choice. This prospect hovers over me like a pterodactyl. Luc does his best to put my mind at ease but I can tell he's frightened, too, and so we're playing a ping-pong game of mutual reassurance, which neither of us really wants to win.

* * *

Putting on a conspiratorial air, Luc stated that he needed to speak to me about urgent matters and dragged me off with him towards the west, all the way to the first escarpments of the Gigots. Once he'd made sure there were no inquisitive eavesdroppers about, he told me he'd given the situation a lot of thought: since the doctors proved to be incapable of waking my mother up and the gimmicks of science remained as ineffective as those of prayer, he recommended using an unconventional method. This prologue aroused my scepticism. What was he going to trot out now? Another crackpot scheme involving tape-recorded train horns and microwave ovens, or some nutty new invention? But he maintained that this time it was serious, totally different. The procedure might fail, of course, but it had to be tried — didn't we have our backs to the wall? He seemed confident he would pull it off. First, he swore me to secrecy about what I was going to see, then he asked me to follow him into the mountains. And I hung on to his footsteps, figuring that, at the very worst, I would finally know what he was up to, all those times he headed for the mountaintop.

Not a single footpath cut through the Gigots. Nobody had cleared one because the place was too forbidding. A mass of gigantic Lego blocks. A procession of carnivorous fractures and mossy crests.

The mosquito kingdom. The perfect spot to hold a Sprain Festival. But Luc had roamed these basalt ridges. He knew their twists and turns, their dead ends; he recognized the traps and boldly thrust his way through. Indifferent to the thornbush's bite, he hauled himself up or slid down, now skirting an insidious crevice lurking beneath a tangle of shrubs, then leaping across another one as jauntily as a young goat. Again and again, he had to wait for me while I stumbled along like a pitiful bug going around in circles in some auto junkyard. Sometimes I thought I was in the nave of a decrepit cathedral, at other times in bombed-out barracks still guarded by stern sentries, and every now and then I seemed to be caught inside the ribcage of a brontosaur which the necrophagous centuries hadn't quite picked clean. The Gigots enclosed and perpetuated one another, and I began to believe their furtive gorges would snake on into infinity. But lo and behold! after christening these new Carpathians with my sweat and satisfying their wee vampires with my blood, after inching along that nasal ledge overlooking dark shards jutting from the waves, after slithering across the brow of a wind-lashed cliff, then climbing one last guano-soiled peak, I received the reward for my efforts. Because down below, hemmed in by the mountains, there lay a tiny cove.

It was a rocky inlet fringed by a tranquil beach of auburn sand. Turquoise waters washed it and large reefs sheltered it against the waves. After the heat, the barrenness, the schizophrenic spruce, nature seemed to let out a sigh, give itself a rest. A treat for the eye. A piece of the tropics that had drifted with the current and ended its long journey here. I followed Luc and clambered down to set foot on the miracle, pulled off my boots and walked on the cove's smooth sand, breathed in its peacefulness, savoured its wild beauty. At the tide line there was a ring of stones from an old fire and a polished tree trunk to sit on. A pretty waterfall drizzled down the mountain face. The cove was a haven, a safe hide-out in the rocky heart of the muscular Gigots, the perfect refuge for a clown like Luc. He led me to the corner of two granite lips that opened into a cave. Wriggling into the fragrant gloom, I found it to be spacious and carpeted with sand. There were candles here and there which Luc did his best to revive, and the cave glowed with light, then with colours, because the ceiling was a fresco that had suddenly been revealed. Vast paintings sprawled over the uneven rock. They were Luc's work. Narwhals mingled with seals; starfish and lobsters drifted whimsically alongside octopuses and rays. Here, porpoises frolicked in seaweed or gamboled in circles above luminous ocean depths, while elsewhere sirenian shepherds rode jellyfish and led their herds of whales to glittering pastures of plankton while, further still, sea monsters clashed in a tangle of snarled tentacles and kraken devoured sharks.

The walls of the cave were lined with wrack. Lying about was a large bag filled with gull feathers, which probably served as a bed. Nearby squatted a coffee table that must have stood in someone's living-room but now held an assortment of paintbrushes and other do-it-yourself tools, as well as seashells, carapaces, fish bones, together with various pieces of jewellery, knick-knacks, and masks created from these materials. At the very back, the cave ended in a kind of alcove steeped in an eerie glow from a flickering paschal candle which seemed to burn continuously. And right next to it, crouching on an altar consisting of flat stones, there was the beast.

A real dragon. A monster armed with claws, a big sinister lizard, the one Luc always drew on everything. That satanic snout, that barbed mouth, and that crest running like a gap-toothed comb all the way to the tip of its tail. The reptile didn't move. It kept still inside its chain mail, and that was to be expected since it wasn't really alive. The saurian was mounted. Stuffed. The mocking smile that seemed to play on its muzzle was fixed for all time. Only the marbles of its gaze sparkled brightly.

'It's the iguana,' Luc whispered in my ear. 'It's a magical animal.'

At first, I thought it had to be a practical joke, but Luc was as solemn as a dozen popes. I leaned forward to take a closer look. I had seen this sort of creepy-crawly before on TV: a marine iguana from the Galápagos Islands.

Coloured pebbles were placed all around, like so many offerings...

11

Clown's Cove is like a song of praise, a solution to the complex equation of the elements. Here, time is only measured by the great clepsydra, and ordinary customs don't apply. We go around stark naked if we want to, deck ourselves out with strings of shells, don helmets of kelp, and laze about as much as we like. We cheer the most thrilling waves, climb the rock face, or putter around quietly inside the cave. We often go swimming. We'll swim around the reefs, beneath eroded cliffs, and at high tide we can dive from the ledges. The Cove is a carapace of clouds, a bunker of blue sky reality simply can't penetrate. It's an enclave of freedom, a place to romp about in the sun and play with the sea. But it's also a reptile's lair, since there is that iguana dwelling in its heart.

What a weird piece of junk that iguana is. He certainly wasn't hatched yesterday. He's a tough nut, a kind of galvanized old punk, although well preserved for his age. If you dropped him in the middle of his old stomping ground in the Galápagos, you might think he was still basking in the sun between two swims. You almost expect to see him leap up and slip away between your legs. That vitality the animal radiates comes especially from its eyes.

Those pupils of pulverized bronze you'd swear you can see quivering; those glowing coals; those tiny, distorting mirrors. They are only glass marbles but seem to blaze with life. No matter where you are in the cave, you feel those eyes fixing on you, following your every move as watchfully as those that stare out at you from the walls of old manor houses. Perched at the centre of an energy field the iguana generates himself, he holds you in his spell. He is a kind of thermostat of the general weirdness around whom everything seems to revolve and, looking at him sitting enthroned on his altar like that, you can easily imagine him to be invested with supernatural powers.

He comes from Mona Daigneault's place. It's a rented iguana with an option to buy, since that's the deal Luc made with the voluptuous widow. It's why he does those odd jobs for her; he is paying the amphibian's rent. Last year, after her taxidermist husband's fatal coronary, Mona hired Luc to do various manual tasks, and while he cleaned the garage, a disaster area whose many strata yielded a wealth of surprises, Luc happened upon the iguana which was pinned between a moose head and a tortoise shell. How the reptile was snatched from his native reef, and on what latter-day *Beagle* he crossed the high seas before ending up in the garage the late Conrad Daigneault used to call his taxidermic museum, will perhaps always remain a mystery.

But what is absolutely certain, on the other hand, is that the moment Luc spotted it, he felt a shock of recognition. I can understand why: that extraterrestrial look they both have, the same remoteness, the same hankering after the water. Would a dissection reveal identical guts? Unfortunately this cannot be verified since the iguana was gutted a long time ago, but Luc tells me he instantly felt the power of their affinity, the truth of this supernatural twinning. He knew right away he had stumbled upon a kindred spirit, a fellow loner, but what ultimately swayed him and confirmed his intention to adopt the saurian, was its knowledge of dreams.

He says the iguana is a dream machine, a visionary instrument, a magic tool that allows you to travel around within your dreams. He claims the reptile has the ability to create holes in the thin membrane separating the real world from the one your mind inhabits during sleep. The iguana is a kind of receiver, he explains, and all you need to do is tune it in, a bit like a radio, to get vivid, freaky dreams — wild, multi-coloured night visions that grab you, send you into raptures, feed your soul. Dreams that illuminate other dreams or themselves. And he's offering me the benefit of this fantastic dream machine. He wants me to use it to get in touch with my mother. He asks me to venture into the shadowland of dreams, to go in search of Mama, and learn from her how she can be restored to life: this is what he proposes.

I have trouble swallowing it, though. Really, an

ancient lizard stuffed with straw and old Chilean newspapers. How can I buy into that? And yet there are those sparks, those eyes shining with a mineral intelligence in the half-light of the cave. The way they glow quietly in the gloom, like a sleeping TV ready to be zapped. There's that smile lingering on the iguana's mouth, as if he were savouring some private joke.

* * *

Luc says there is a great deal of coherence, a sequential order, in the dreams the iguana transmits — they are like daily instalments of a serial in which you play the lead. He himself is reborn every night into an underwater world. He dreams he is a kind of man-fish, a merman perfectly adapted to that oceanic universe. And he has a tongue-twisting name: something that sounds like 'Fngl.' At least, that's what his fellow sea creatures call him, because Fngl isn't the only merman on the block. In this sensuous fantasy sea, there are other water beings wheeling about, whom Luc calls 'gliders' in contrast to us 'plodders,' poor humans that we are, weighed down by the gravity of our land-bound condition. Luc tells me the gliders are pilgrims, adventurers, or simply wanderers. He encounters them at the crossing of two currents or at a bend in a liquid path, and then they sing and hunt together and compete in mind-boggling swimming tournaments, or they will

79

chatter about profound matters in oceanic caverns, where dreams emerge and forms converge, or vanish into the distant deep.

So this explains the gibberish and other watery conversations that spark up his sleep.

12

Now I know what inspires his fluty language and the Egyptoid poems he commits to paper. It's a glider thing. The same goes for his drawings: what Luc sees and experiences in his dreams, he tries to illustrate, to paint. It's from these visions that springs his great fresco of the deep, a work he is hoping, perhaps, to pass on to future generations of oddballs, a composition that will no doubt provoke the astonishment, if nothing else, of archaeologists in the year 5000.

The origin of his obsession with underwater breathing is no longer a mystery; I know where it comes from. But what isn't clear is where it will lead him, for he finds breathing in the water of his nightly dreams *so* exhilarating that he has decided to do likewise while awake. He's analysing the mechanism, the feeling, and trying to duplicate them. He is conducting experiments. Two or three times a day, he actually drowns himself and pukes up litres of ocean, but that doesn't faze him; he still thinks it can be done. His resolve is like tempered steel — he wants to revive the forgotten traditions of his gill-bearing ancestors. He honestly thinks he'll succeed, and it's a waste of time to remind him he is only a mammal, that even whales need air. He claims he has pinpointed the basic problem. That

blasted muscular reflex locking the windpipe to prevent drowning: this is what one needs to control. As
well as developing more strength in the thorax area
to make it easier to expel water. With this goal in
mind, he subjects himself to an exercise programme.
From an old inner tube he has molded a corset he
forces himself to wear for at least an hour every day
in order to increase the size and strength of his chest
muscles. He figures this discipline will produce the
desired effect. He truly believes in this freaky iguana
stuff at the Cove. He has actually more faith in it, I
think, than in the drab reality prevailing outside his
hideaway, but the worst is that it seems to be contagious. Perhaps I've flipped my lid without noticing,
for I, too, am tempted to believe in it even though
it makes no sense. It's just that, in the Cove, reason
doesn't carry the same weight as it does everywhere
else. Other powers are at work here. For a start,
that of the lizard snoozing in the cave. The iguana
sends a thrill through my soul. Every time I come to
the Cove, I am swept up in the magic of the place
and feel a great rush of joy. It's as though wonderful
things were ready to happen, as though a void was
about to be filled. In the past, I would have made fun
of all this and labelled Luc a madman, but the events
of the last couple of months have opened my mind
to other possibilities…

* * *

My encyclopedia is silent on the most important issue: not a single word on how to tune in a Galápagos iguana. So I have to rely on Luc. I do my best to imitate him. I place pebbles on the altar, as he does, then crouch down on a kelp mat in an attitude of prayer. Because we've gone back to *that* now; like the Big Guy Up There, the lizard feeds on prayer. There's no getting around it.

I open myself up to the iguana. I try to decipher the meaning of his smile, but it seems to change with the light — sometimes I feel I'm dealing with a mischievous gnome, at other times with a wise man weighed down by the years. There are also strange visions, mirages. This morning, I thought I saw my father's features slipping over the iguana's crepey face, but I was probably just imagining things. Kneeling on my rug of dried seaweed, I look up at the lizard, focus my thoughts, and wait for something to happen. It would be easier without the hummingbird, that invisible little creature who never fails to show up and buzz around my ears, snickering at my naïveté. Soon I feel like a fool and can't stand it anymore: I need to go out then and busy myself with something concrete, something less futile, such as taking an inventory of the Cove's grains of sand. From a technical viewpoint, Luc doesn't know how to advise me, since communicating with the iguana is instinctive with him. He has never needed to learn how. He plunges into it as if it were a deliciously inviting tropical lagoon, and the rest takes care of itself. So I have to fend for myself and attempt to find on my own the directions, the open sesame, the appropriate prayer. I am searching, I try different tricks. I recycle old litanies:

Our Iguana who art so ugly,
Thy will be done in my head as it is in heaven.
Thy dreams come...

* * *

Fngl's mother is a mermaid a human fisherman caught in his net one day and subjected to an unnatural embrace. Fngl, the result of that involuntary union, was born on the shore like a sea turtle and spent his squalid childhood years among plodders. But as he grew up, the biological legacy of his glider ancestry expressed itself: a metamorphosis took place — he discovered his aquatic skills, understood his true nature. Then, finally, at the age of twelve, he returned to the sea. Ever since that second birth, Fngl has tirelessly criss-crossed the briny deep in search of the naiad who bore him in her womb. Having learned of the existence of an underwater city called Ftan, where the nation of mermaids and mermen are rumoured to dwell, he set off, excitedly thrashing the waves, but the route to the town is a hazardous one, since the wondrous Shimmering City isn't situated at a fixed point in the ocean. It moves about, drifts along with the currents, travels, changes place continuously. Fngl has yet to catch sight of the ten-drilled town's sargasso train. Every single night the challenge of finding it returns, yet he doesn't despair. As he clashes with sea monsters but also marvels at bewitching sights and discovers sunken treasures, he continues his quest.

This is the tale Luc tells me while the fire crackles away. And I listen, amazed, dazzled by his power-ful imagination, but fascinated as well by what he doesn't mention: the obvious similarity between his fable and reality, the close resemblance between him and Fngl. When Luc recounts the young merman's adventures, he always does so in the first person and sounds as if he were speaking from experience, as though he were describing his own world, his own destiny, as though he straddled two equally concrete lives. I wonder how deeply rooted this split is in his mind. Does he honestly believe that Fngl's story is *his* story? That he's the hybrid fruit of a pig and a mermaid? That his mother has returned to her native seas? Is this how he explains why her body was never recovered? He wouldn't dare admit it, of course, but I know he's practically convinced it is so. That's why he scans the dark waves night after night. He longs to hear a certain song. He is waiting for the mermaid's call. *She* is the reason he dances at the water's edge to ward off the winds. *She* is the one he thinks about when he gazes out at the swells in his iguana crouch.

13

I've started sleeping again. It wasn't easy. At first I just couldn't because I'd lost the habit. I would back gingerly into sleep with shivery eyelids, afraid I might tumble into Kilometre 54 the way you slip into a wolverines' lair. Nothing of the kind happened, though. The Kilometre's apparitions have stopped. The blizzard, the yellow eye, the horn, the frantic flight through the terrifying maze — it's all gone. Since I have no reason anymore to practise insomnia, I sink luxuriously into sleep like a bear in winter. Actually, I may be sleeping too well, for I am getting only ordinary dreams. None of them seems to have anything to do with Mama. Does this mean the iguana is simply a hollow hide, a puppet filled with untrue news stories? Better not say this to Luc, because he fiercely defends the saurian. Rather than admitting that the stuffed critter is incompetent, he chooses to lay the blame on me. He tells me my faith in it isn't strong enough.

* * *

I sleep like a log and regain my long-lost strength, but in the land of dreams all is dead quiet. To remedy this deficiency, Luc has decided to teach me to dance. It's a good way to become receptive to the iguana, he feels. The dance is part of glider lore. Fngl learned it from a merman, an old conger-eel breeder, and Luc has adapted it, designed a plodder version for his own use. The dance is believed to have magical properties. Its practice supposedly invests you with the power to control the elements, master the currents, to lull storms or cause them, should the need arise. Luc insists on tutoring me in its basic principles. He says the dance will boost my confidence, kick-start my languid faith, and he urges me to put my heart and soul into it, but it's not that simple. Appearances notwithstanding, there's more to the ritual than sticking fishbones into your hair and hopping about excitedly in the waves while uttering a series of yelps and squeals. There's a complex choreography involved. There are those barks you have to know how to modulate, and especially that looseness you need to aim for, that unforced ease. In order for it to work, Luc says, you must have the right intention — that of not having any. Quite a contortionist's act for the mind — trying to concentrate while going with the flow.

* * *

He accuses me of laziness. He desperately wants me to dance, presses me to give it at least a try. I wriggle my shins just to please him and venture a few steps, try a couple of clucks, then I stop, feeling embarrassed. It's no good: I watch him dislocating his kneecaps and jumping about like a chicken without a head while yapping into the sea breeze, but to me it simply looks like a weird kind of rock 'n' roll. He blames me for my lack of stick-to-it-iveness, but has he any idea about the sceptical hummingbird that has a ringside seat and noisily jeers at all my huffing and puffing? Luc keeps saying it's a cinch — all you have to do is let your mind go blank and relax, as with a circus trick. He says dancing is like cycling, you just have to get the hang of it, but who is *he* to draw such a parallel, since he doesn't even own a scooter?

* * *

They are going to move Mama to Quebec City. They say it has become necessary, and my grandfolks tell me they have given permission to have her admitted to that blasted clinic in the capital. They are going to take her there five days from now, in a flying ambulance. They may as well send her to the moon.

* * *

I've dreamt about her. I walked into her room, but it wasn't the Villeneuve hospital room anymore. This was a dark, medieval chamber, and beyond the window a rainy sky bore down on the verdigris gables of Quebec City's old quarter. My mother's bed was an antique, monumental affair, with long curtains of frayed voile spilling down from its canopy. She rested peacefully on this catafalque but her hair was a tangle of icicles. Her cheeks were hollow, her features wasted. An unimaginable stretch of time had shrivelled and withered her. Mama seemed to have been sleeping for ages in this dungeon and had turned into a mummified shadow of her former self. I woke up in the stillness that precedes the gulls' raucous serenades and my very first thought was about the iguana. Could this possibly be the dream I was told to expect?

* * *

The apparition still haunted me when we went to visit Mama, and when I saw the dreadful wizened mask imprint itself on her face, it suddenly struck me that the dream was premonitory: I had seen Mama as she was going to be if nothing were done to wake her up. I knew right then and there that it would be a serious mistake to ship her off to Quebec City and we must pull her out of that bed without further delay or she would remain in limbo forever. We needed to bring her home; I was painfully certain of it, and my conviction was so strong I had no trouble communicating it. Luc declared the idea was simply brilliant and Grandmother rallied to it, too — what better place for Mama to come alive again than in her childhood home?

Once we had tracked down Dr. Longuet at the outpatient clinic, we told him what we wished to do, but he put a damper on our enthusiasm. He didn't think a premature discharge would improve Mama's condition. He considered it necessary to send her to Quebec City where she would get the best treatment available. Oh, what a pill this bumptious medic was, speaking to us as if he were addressing a kindergarten class! But his words shook Grandmother's resolve and, when we found ourselves back in the corridor, she was inclined to agree with the Stethoscopian: after all, how much value did a flash of intuition really have, compared to the huge amount of knowledge washing over representatives of the medical profession from morning till night? I wasn't going to be fobbed off with these superstitions, though. I knew I was right, and gave Grandmother a good tongue-lashing, accusing her of letting herself be hornswoggled by the doctor. When she saw how angry I was, she seemed to waver and admitted she needed Grandfather's opinion. While she went off to phone him, we headed for the cafeteria where we knocked back an orange pop, and I was relieved to hear that Luc agreed with me. We saw eye to eye: since the clinician's unwholesome influence was paralysing Grandmother's will, we were going to take action. And we mobilized our neuronal resources in order to work out an abduction plan.

We would kidnap Mama at lunchtime. In some far-off corridor, Luc would rivet everyone's attention

by pretending he was having a fit of demonic possession, and I would take advantage of that diversion to
seize hold of my mother. I would put her in a wheelchair and slip out through a basement door. The
good old bungalow of my former life was only two
blocks away and I still had the key: it would make a
wonderful hideout. We were well aware of the haz-
ards of such an operation. We knew we needed to
fool the staff, that I might be recognized and chased
after while piloting my mother through the premises.
In a scenario worthy of a demolition derby, I already
had visions of myself tearing along corridors that
bristled with traps and narrowly escaping from our
pursuers by leaping from elevator to elevator. I was
propelling Mama across the packed cafeteria while
lunch trays flew in every direction and a squadron of
white-coated musclemen hunted us down. I pictured
us being surrounded, cornered in the laundry room,
entrenched at last between two rows of gigantic
washing machines, hostile science-fiction Buddhas
with gaping bellies. No doubt about it, the venture
was fraught with danger, yet we needed to give it a
try since it was vitally important. As midday drew
near, however, and adrenaline flooded through our
veins, Grandmother came back, and we saw that
she had completely regained her fighting spirit. She
announced that Grandfather supported us unreserv-
edly. Invigorated by this approval, she marched us
off to the administrative offices where we burst in
on the director.

He wasn't exactly pleased to see us. He sent for Longuet as a reinforcement, and together they justified their rejection of our request by dishing up an indigestible stew of medical and administrative arguments. But we weren't going to let them intimidate us, and Grandmother kept insisting that the fruit of her womb be returned to her. The explosive entry of a dishevelled Grandfather, who dictatorially clamoured for an ambulatory treatment, was all that was needed to tip the scales. Since Mama's condition didn't present any particular cause for concern in a medical sense, it was decreed we would be granted permission to look after her in our home environment and, after the signing of a great flurry of forms, she was given back to us. I had won.

They delivered her to us by silent ambulance and we settled her in the room that had been her bedroom when she was a girl, which is next to mine. We are going to take such good care of her! We'll show those medics and nurses what we're capable of. They'll find out what tender loving care can accomplish. In the warm bosom of her family, with our combined affectionate vibrations enveloping her, it won't be long, I'm sure, before Mama opens her eyes again.

14

Mama's homecoming has transformed the house into a quiet hive of activity. We take turns at her bedside. Her nearness boosts my spirits, to say nothing of hope, an added bonus. I take really good care of my beautiful rescued mother and try to awaken her senses. I have her smell the scent of her favourite flowers. I sit and chat, I read to her, play music she likes, and every morning I open her window so she can hear the refrain of the sea. Luc fusses over her with equal devotion. He would sleep at the foot of her bed if it were allowed. He surrounds her with mystical shells and whispers certain healing formulas to her in merman jargon.

* * *

On the verandah, Luc and Grandfather are discussing the weather forecast in teeth-clicking code with the earnestness of a pair of shrewd old salts. Luc managed to get himself invited to the smokehouse today, which just shows how much trust the old man puts in him. As for Grandmother, she still occasionally jumps when she happens to meet him coming around a corner of some hallway, but she offers him our unconditional hospitality: Luc is welcome to sleep at our place whenever he wants and eat here any time. In order to be worthy of this honour, he tries to become domesticated. He's acquainting himself with the use of a comb and does his best to penetrate the mysteries of the rules of etiquette. He never lets an opportunity slip by to praise Grandmother's cooking to the skies or make an appreciative comment on what she happens to be wearing. She is sensitive to such courtesies and gazes at him with an increasingly benevolent expression in her eyes, wondering, perhaps, if concealed beneath that crude attire, there might actually lurk a gentleman. Luc has a knack for worming his way into our daily habits. You should see him sipping his tea in the living room with Grandmother. He's not being hypocritical — he really enjoys it, he says.

* * *

In spite of our vigilant care and attention, Mama continues to waste away. I had thought that, for her eyes to open, we only needed to replant her in a favourable compost, but I'm forced to accept that our titanic affection isn't enough. Luc says we need to pray to the iguana. In his opinion, the dream about the mummy — that enlightening vision I had — was engineered by the saurian. He is delighted the dream machine worked despite the hummingbird's ploys, and he views the iguana's spontaneous demonstration of his powers as an exceptional favour. He feels it's a sign of good will, an invitation to believe. I question this analysis but it seems foolish to rule out that the amphibian may have influenced things, and since I really don't want to take any chances, I'll begin stomping afresh tomorrow on the Cove's cinnamon sands. My tongue may get sunburned, but I'll keep chanting at the top of my voice:

Hail Iguana full of straw,
The dancer sweats with thee.
Blessed art thou amongst animals,
And blessed is the seller of thy hide, Mona.

* * *

Kilometre 54 caught me by surprise as it flung open a whistling gate onto its pitch-black squalls and slashed me with icy knives. The howling walls and the maze were gone, but it had to be the Kilometre since rails stretched out at my feet. Improbable lamps pierced the blizzard. I realized they were searchlights belonging to the rescue party. For, as I gathered from the bits and pieces of mechanical parts and snow-mobile fragments that lay scattered about, I stood at the exact spot where the accident had happened. The train itself was nowhere to be seen, but I pictured it crouching in the heart of the darkness. Braving the storm's throbbing blades, I followed the track like a haggard railway-man. Numb with cold, I staggered on in the gale, then I noticed a pink form in the snow. Pink like Mama's Ski-doo suit. Her body lying in a snowdrift. I rushed over and knelt down beside her. She lay slumped like a doll tossed there by some giant child. I took off her helmet and her hair coiled around my wrists. She was asleep. I called her as loudly as I could, but she went on sleeping, and while I desperately tried to revive her, I suddenly felt a presence. A shadow eclipsed the searchlights. In the eye of the maelstrom loomed a figure.

The unexpected visitor had no head, and magma of living ink oozed from his lacerated neck. It was my decapitated father. He towered at the Kilometre's centre as if he were its soul, and the winds bowed down at his feet. He came nearer, displacing patches of darkness, but I drew back because of the blasts of terror escorting him and the furious whirlwinds rotating towards me. The ghost pushed me away from my mother, then positioned himself between us, shielding Mama with his body. Suddenly I knew. I understood *he* was the one who held Mama prisoner. He was making her stay with him, keeping her for himself. He made sure she didn't wake up, didn't go back to us. Bending down over my poor mother, he lifted her up as easily as if she were a pink flamingo, then carried her off, dissolving with his burden into the raging blackness. So *Papa* was the jailer of Kilometre 54?

Luc was there when I surfaced in my icy bed, and I gave him a detailed report of my inner adventure. He wanted me to go back to sleep right away

and return to that place so I might get to the heart
of the matter, but the mere thought petrified me.
Hadn't the phantom made it clear he considered
me an intruder? Hadn't he barred me from entering the Kilometre? Who am I to challenge a father's
ghostly authority?

* * *

I would gladly revert to my old insomniac self, but
Luc declares running away doesn't solve anything. I
know he is right. I have no choice. I have a mother to
save. So I must return to the Kilometre since there's
no other way. I need to see the nightmare through to
the end and have it out with the ghost. I must clarify
his intentions and negotiate Mama's release.

Holy Iguana, with eyes so odd,
Protect me, the dreamer,
Now, from the fear of my dad.

* * *

I thought I had stepped into the wrong dream, for
there was no blizzard whipping across the white
plain. The sky was the bottom of a bottle that dis-
torted the stars. I saw the ghost at once, standing in
this wilderness of snow with Mama stretched out at
his feet. He stood quite still. And remained still. And
since he kept holding this immobile pose, I dared to

97

go nearer. He continued to loom motionless. A deactivated robot. A statue plunked down in the middle of the great white void. Except for that condensing breath, that frosted mist rising from his jagged neck. As inconspicuously as I could, I crouched down beside Mama who slept in the shadow of this phantom tree, and I whispered her name. I called her softly so she'd wake up and we could run away together far from the terrible guard. Because she didn't respond, I began shaking her, and this is when the ghost awakened. He grew to an enormous size, and from the gaping tunnel of his neck sprang the blizzard. I was knocked flat, sent rolling over the frozen plain, flung out of the dream, back to the hollow of my bed. Expelled. Punished for my audacity.

Why this hostility? What happened to the affection, the closeness, the harmony there once was between us? Luc believes the ghost doesn't recognize me, but I'm sure he's wrong. Papa knows who I am; we just don't see eye to eye anymore — *that* is the problem.

* * *

Two nights later. After a few disastrous experiences, I think I've found a way to mollify the ghost. It can be done, provided one doesn't attempt to take Mama away from him. He lets me go near her, and I'm even allowed to touch her if I want, but when I try to wake her up, he cloaks himself in icy blasts and chases me from the Kilometre. Otherwise, if I keep quiet, he is tolerant. Indifferent, actually. He ignores me. He just sits there doing nothing. Or walks around us like a sentry. I know he is watching me even though he pretends he isn't, but I don't think I have anything to fear so long as I play by his rules.

15

Kilometre 54 is a myriad of snowscapes woven into one. It has a life of its own, a fluttering fringe. It is crowded with different moments — now gloomy, now peaceful, but always new, and sometimes fragrant as a December morning. The days can be pale, dim, overcast, the nights sparkling and silky. The blizzard is only the spot's sternest face. I have an inkling the Kilometre responds to the ghost's many moods, adapts to them, feeds on them. Unless it's the other way around. There exists in any case an umbilical connection between the two, a symbiotic relationship. The ghost himself isn't mean, after all. He looks terrifying but turns out to be harmless. He pays no attention to me, doesn't seem to hear anything I say to him. He lets me trudge along by his side when he decides to carry Mama for hours on end in the shattered night, following the rails without ever reaching the scarlet moon, without ever arriving anywhere... This is what the ghost is like, he is the very image of the Kilometre: full of vast empty spaces — insane, lethal, but nonetheless, in his own way, magnanimous.

* * *

Not a puff of wind disturbed the stillness of the immaculate white expanse, and legions of airborne flakes drifted lazily down. The ghost held Mama in his arms and rocked her as if she were a little child. He stroked her brow, her hair, and his gestures were suffused with gentleness. I think he would have kissed her had he been able to, and suddenly his intentions were revealed to me in a new light. Could the motive for his jealous watch over my mother simply be love? Is my father incapable of parting from his beloved? Is that why he holds her captive? How can I hope to persuade him then to surrender her to me? And first of all, how am I to make myself heard by this melancholy phantom who has no ears to listen with, and even less a mouth through which he might reply? By what means are we to communicate? Using Morse code? Telepathy?

* * *

You'd almost think the ghost wants to take the initiative. Last night, when I reached the Kilometre, I found him waiting for me at the edge of the railway bed. He seemed agitated, singularly aware of my presence. Shedding the supreme reserve that had marked his behaviour until then, he addressed me through gestures. His arms spread in a helpless manner, encompassing the Kilometre, then his mittens fell off and his hands reached out to me. It was a gesture the son of the Guy who Runs the Show could have made when asking the little children to come to him, except that I happened to be the only kid around and rather reluctant to honour the invitation. Papa's hands rose, flew up to the huge void of his face. Then, out of his gaping neck leapt a tongue of fire. This flame danced about on his shoulders and coiled within its own spiralling wreaths, taking on the crude shape of the head that had once been there. It was like a pulpy mass of molten metals in which emerged the grimacing shadow of an anguished face. The hands moved away from this burning visage and swept imploringly towards me. Insistent. Beseeching. Then they beat the frigid air like startled gulls and soared away moments before the dream evaporated.

This was the first time the ghost shed his armour of indifference and tried to start a dialogue. His intentions remain unclear and the purpose of the dream unfathomable, but I have a feeling that a new chapter in the history of our phantom-and-son relationship has just begun.

* * *

I am visited by new bursts of night visions that are difficult to describe but must surely be coming from my father since they all conjure up the same thing: his hands, his face. I glimpse blazing features, mutant heads of lava, and other eruptive sproutings. Time and again, I am implored by hands that open and reach out to me. I think the ghost may be struggling to convey a message. What is the meaning of these cryptic pantomimes and insane cremations? What is he trying to get me to understand?

* * *

The visions are feverish. Some are quite horrifying, like that paternal face being gobbled up all the way to the bone by famished worms, while others are merely strange, haunting: Papa's visage turning into an impossible jigsaw puzzle whose pieces won't stay in place and vanish one by one. A photo in which the features begin to shimmy, then become so muddled they are unrecognizable. His portrait chalked on a sidewalk washed by rain. The empty wake of his gaze swallowed up by the ocean...

* * *

The ghost is growing impatient. His appearances are no longer confined to the realm of dreams but encroach alarmingly upon reality. The visions poke through my lashes in the iridescent glow of dawn and assail me even in broad daylight. I hallucinate. I see hands forming on the white surface of clouds. Papa's grimace hovers in a curtain as it billows in the breeze, looms up in the golden dust filtering from a window. Even the moon is mixed up in it, stretching out imploring hands to me with the hint of a gaze melting on its round face.

Those hands, those fluid faces, those ill omens, images that whirl briefly in the wind and are gone...

* * *

I feel I'm being watched. I dare not look in the mirror anymore for fear of glimpsing a headless figure behind me. What is the point of these livid mime hands, as white as Mickey's gloves, flitting about in black light, then opening out like poisonous flowers? What am I to make of these heads of dripping clay blazing up and writhing on my father's bare shoulders? It is a code whose key eludes me. I don't know what he is driving at. I just don't understand, and that unnerves me. Luc doesn't give up, though. He thinks there has to be a reason for these hauntings. He is convinced my visions mean something. He insists on my describing them in detail for him and analyses it all, doing his best to pull the main thread out of this tangled skein. Tirelessly, he struggles to sort out what to me is nothing but a jumble.

* * *

Luc has reached certain conclusions. He thinks he has figured out what my father is trying to convey to me: he wants me to return his head to him.

The hypothesis is nutty beyond words but does

have the merit of fitting the facts into a coherent scheme. Luc thinks Papa is a prisoner of Kilometre 54, that he's bored to tears there and keeps Mama with him so he won't be lonely. Luc supposes he would willingly release her if he could break away from that purgatory himself and attain the rest owing the dead, but he cannot do this. According to Luc, Papa can't escape from the Kilometre because he is incomplete, because his head is missing. Therefore, the solution is obvious: we need to return it to him. Luc thinks he has been asking for this all along; the visions and all those imploring gestures are to be interpreted in this way. In his opinion, there's no question about it: my father wants me to help him find his head. An impossible task, on the face of it, since his head was annihilated by the train. But is there any real proof that it was crushed? I have always been convinced my father's skull was destroyed because this is what I was told, but what are the known facts?

* * *

I have subjected my grandfolks to a close interrogation. They were baffled and somewhat disturbed by my questions but answered them to the best of their ability. As far as they knew, the head was indeed shattered. At least, this was the conclusion reached by the police officers involved in the investigation, because they could find no trace of if. But now that

I stop to think about it, the assumption strikes me as rather improbable. It must have been difficult to conduct a thorough search when winter held the fifty-fourth kilometre in its arctic grip. What if, instead of being crushed, Papa's head had only been severed? What if it had been hurled into the air and had landed at some distance in the deep snow, thus escaping the officers' attention?

* * *

Once upon a time, my venerable forefather chose a lonely place away from the village to bury his dead, and that same spot, on the hill, is still the site of Ferland's cemetery. Big, leafy trees grow there and their bows form an openwork archway over the tombs. When I entered this lacy cathedral, I was surprised to see how thick the grass on my father's grave already was. I came to look for a sign, some sort of confirmation, and I questioned his epitaph for a long time, but it remained silent. Unless, of course, one counts as a reply the rustling of the leaves, the creak of branches stirred by breaths of ocean air, and those quiet sobs drifting up from the trees — the ethereal sighing of the wind.

16

Boudine, the notary's son, agreed to rent his motorbike to me for five hundred humbugs, gas not included. Luc loaded an extra fuel can onto his back and, after a spluttering three-hour ride on the hinterland's gangways, the fifty-fourth kilometre revealed itself to us in its true, vaguely radioactive light. A sky dotted with timid fleecy clouds. A picture-postcard bush. At long last, I saw the setting of the tragedy with my own eyes. It had all happened right there, between the iron bridge that stretched across the river and the difficult curve oozing from the north. A great spot for skidooing, providing you added snow, then superimposed the shadowy light of a winter's evening and summoned up a murderous north wind. But it was hard to envision the place like that on this scorching August morning, with the sun making our caps stick to our heads and swarms of miniature choppers attacking us. Frightened at first by our arrival, the birds soon went back to twittering and the crickets to crittering in the narrow strip of swampy ground. We anointed ourselves with fly oil, then began our search under the impious gaze of the crows, those negative gulls. We meant to scour the area around the railway line, but also the tall grass and the edge of the forest — rugged stretches of wasteland where the head could easily have been catapulted. I was trying not to think about what I might find. I only hoped the local necrophagous life forms had had the time to finish their job.

We were advancing into enemy territory, because this was the train's dominion. Walking along the rails was like following the monster's fresh tracks, and I moved cautiously forward with nerves as taut as an anchor rope in a stormy sea. My insides churned with rage. I wished it dared to show itself, that scrap heap, that mangler of fathers, so I could vent my vengeful fury and pepper the monster with stones and abuse. I felt like setting a trap for it, removing the bolts from the rails or blowing up the pillars of the bridge. How sorry I was I didn't have the necessary tools with me! Now, all I could do was pelt the detested track with my spit.

We came across traces of the accident here and there: Plexiglas splinters and fragments of fibreglass, mechanical parts, shreds of a saddle. Then a whole ski oddly planted in the bushes like some cabalistic sign. Luc suddenly called out to me and I crossed the track. I prepared myself for the worst. But it wasn't the head. It was one of my mother's mittens. I put this relic in my bag and we beat the undergrowth even more zealously. We were convinced the object of our quest was close by.

Never, ever, would the fifty-fourth kilometre be scanned with greater precision than by our young, radar-like senses. Yet the day drew to a close without us finding even my father's helmet, and we ended up near the bridge empty-handed, mortified. We got home at dusk. We were so dirty Grandmother almost had a fit, but after a series of thorough scrubbings she agreed nevertheless to feed us. Luc decided to stay overnight.

He's right there, heaped on top of the other bed like a pile of caviar, snoring away while I write. What has happened to the head? Was it pinched by an animal? Did a wolf or bear make off with Papa's skull to savour it quietly in the comfort of his lair? And what am I supposed to do now?

* * *

It must have been midnight or thereabouts when Luc's aquatic gibberish woke me up. He was jabbering with some merman he knows. I got up to go to the bathroom and, as I walked by Mama's room, I noticed the door was ajar. I went in to make sure everything was all right. A tranquil moon hovered in the window, blanketing Mama with an extra eiderdown. I was just going to leave when something caught my eye: by the foot of the bed, the floor glistened. The boards were wet. There were even puddles. Footprints. With my blood running cold, I turned towards the darkest corner of the room and found myself staring at Papa.

He was terribly real in his Ski-doo suit with that melted snow dripping from his boots. Out of the volcanic crater of his neck rose an icy exhalation that condensed into a ghostly face. I would have liked to believe he was only here to visit my mother, but when I saw his hands reaching towards me, I knew he had come to get his head.

'I couldn't find it,' I gasped out. 'We searched everywhere, but it wasn't there.'

I tried hard to think of an excuse, an explanation. I wanted the phantom to realize it wasn't my fault, but his hands remained extended, insistent, and from his fingers radiated cold waves that twisted my stomach into a tight knot. He started to move. He came towards me, making the floorboards creak beneath his unearthly weight, and it was no longer to implore that he stretched out his fingers, but to demand. I was stiff as a poker, unable to run away while the hands lengthened to catch me and a warm snake slid down my leg, slithering away through my pajama bottoms...

Suddenly, I was back in my bed, with Luc smothering my screams. He explained it was a nightmare and ordered me to be quiet before I alerted the whole household. I managed to control myself although the darkness around me crawled with living things. My sheets were wet with urine, but at this point sleeping was out of the question anyway. We threw on our clothes, slipped out of the house, and headed for the Cove to consult the iguana. Because the ghost will definitely return tonight. And again tomorrow night, and the night after that. He will keep coming back for as long as he needs to. I have no choice; I must find a way to give him what he wants.

17

After a hellish morning spent racking our brains, we finally thought of a solution: we were going to make a duplicate head. We had no other option, since the original article couldn't be found. At least we would be taking action rather than giving in to apathy.

Everything we needed, I found in the attic, in the cupboard where Grandmother keeps her wigs from the sixties. A dozen synthetic scalps were gathering dust up there, and I simply picked one, also taking along the Styrofoam head that served as its stand. At the Cove, the handyman tools were waiting for me on the little table, laid out like surgical instruments, and we got down to work, trimming, gluing, and combing like fanatical do-it-yourselfers. I soon realized that achieving a likeness wasn't essential. What needed to be done was to win the ghost over by presenting him with an extraordinary object, and not irritate him with a bad copy. And since the project was an artistic one, we unleashed the full force of our imaginations, losing all track of time until the evening hour, when the curious sun bent down to cast a ray into our cave.

I have before me the result of our inspired exertions. It is a dazzling golden head. The cheeks are backs of sea-urchins, the pupils tiny pebbles, and enamelled shells serve as ears. We have painted it a bright gold, embellished it with arabesques, topped it with feathers before encircling it with a wreath of whalebone. It looks like a precious mask belonging to the pharaoh of some underwater realm. This head is truly magnificent. Even the iguana seems impressed. What remains to be seen is whether the ghost will accept it...

* * *

A canopy of branches concealed the cemetery from the moon's inquisitive gaze. The Ancients' tall, elaborate cross towered over that spot like a scarecrow over the gums of an enormous gap-toothed mouth. As light-footed as sprites, we noiselessly slipped between the tombstones until we reached my father's, which was frighteningly pale. But the time for shilly-shallying was past and, in the flashlights' self-centred glow, our spades bit into the lawn. Devoid of its crust, the earth responded to the shovels' cold caresses, and we turned into valiant muscle machines, taking care to pace ourselves, working away with the determination of those who have made up their minds to see their task through to the end. One must have exhumed one's father to be able to understand what I felt while the pit was dug and my thoughts deepened along with it. It was as though the massive tapestry of oblivion drew aside, as though the memory of the one who was at the core of things suddenly burst through the surface like a great white whale. Childhood re-emerged, a mosaic of harmonious moments, but of clashes as well — an artesian recalling of insignificant hours, which are ultimately all that matter. Time grew elastic. Now, the only vivid, sparkling thing in that narrow world was the thud of our shovels gutting the fresh earth and ruthlessly slicing through inno-cent earthworms — a cruel necessity we were able to ignore on account of the primordial humus smell and the hypnotic coming together of steel and sweat. A languorous, intoxicating warmth overwhelmed us. I had the strange feeling I was plunging more truly into my inner self than into the depths of the earth, that I was piercing the tendon-like membrane of reality and fleeing from the distant aperture. The earth piled up, rose steadily, but grew heavy none-theless, because the sand, attuned to the seriousness of the occasion, would fall in deliberately. To keep our spirits up and maintain our momentum, we launched into a digging song, the one belonging to miners and moles, to secret philosophies. We didn't worry about anyone hearing us, for the world now ended at the frontiers of that pit in which we toiled.

We were into it all the way up to our eyebrows when, at last, we hit a hard surface. The coffin, the closed door to my father's catacomb. We finished freeing it, then I grabbed hold of a screwdriver.

The tool shook between my fingers. I had difficulty aligning it with the screws but refused Luc's help: opening a father's casket was a sacred task, which only an unworthy son would have the audacity to delegate. The last screw popped out. Since I felt my courage ebbing away, I quickly lifted the lid and we crossed the beams of our flashlights.

Papa was there. Up to the collar, at least. He didn't appear to be in too bad a shape. He even looked rather handsome in his Sunday best. Luc passed me the wig box. I took out the head and held it up to show my father. Respectfully, I laid it down at the upper end of the coffin and wedged it in with stones so it wouldn't roll about. Lying there with his new head, Papa resembled a recumbent statue in its medieval crypt. All he lacked was the noble rocky beard and the large sword: he was like a king with a gold mask, relieved at last of the burden of the ages, dreaming for all eternity. Struck by this Arthurian image, I began humming the *Carmina Burana* overture. Swept along by the music's epic grandeur, I caught myself singing at the top of my lungs. I filled the pit with glorious melodies. I was flying high. My spirits soared. This was the last salute, the final homage to my father, and I didn't want it to stop. Luc tapped me on the shoulder and pointed to the rosy glow in the east. Re-entering the continuum of time, I tightened the screws on Papa's box and we grabbed our shovels, because everything had to be put back into its proper place without delay. We had

115

to piece the grassy puzzle together meticulously: no trace of our digging should remain.

It must have been seven o'clock when we staggered, reeling, into Clown's Cove. We were wrung out but happy, basking in the satisfaction of having done our duty. After a swim in the sea, we went to meditate at the feet of the iguana. We claimed we had no use for sleep, but the strain of our nocturnal journey soon caught up with us and, next to each other, we drifted into a dream suffused with a tropical early-morning radiance. I dreamt about an enormous sun rising on Kilometre 54. Papa stood on the railway track in that blood-red dawn. On his shoulders sparkled the golden head, and I could tell from his smile that the offering had been accepted. I went up to him. He welcomed me and folded me into his powerful warmth. He planted a kiss on my forehead, then turned around and marched off, because the sun was waiting for him. I would have liked to make him stay, or go with him, but I knew I shouldn't. The sun split open like a wound to take him in. Inside, a vast tunnel opened up. At its far end pulsated crimson flashes of soundless lightning. Proudly wearing his new, golden head, Papa strode across the horizon and disappeared into the bowels of the hollow star. And as Kilometre 54 registered the shock of this nuclear daybreak, thousands of crows flew away, scattering in all directions. I woke up crying and slipped out, with the compassionate face of the high arbiter of the skies beaming down on me. Luc came and found me at the water's edge. I was unable to speak but he didn't need to be told anything; he knew the quest for the head was over and that my tears heralded my recovery.

* * *

The most extraordinary part was yet to come. Later, when I got home, I found my grandfolks beside themselves with excitement, completely overwhelmed as they gave me the news that Mama had opened her eyes.

Not even for a minute, a second, or a sigh, but they say she mumbled a few indistinct words before falling asleep again. Her breathing is deep, her pulse can be felt, her skin is warm to the touch. And I know it is thanks to Golden Head. Before migrating to the heart of the sun, he has presented me with this final token of love; he has released Mama and unsealed her eyes. So this is how miracles happen: suddenly, after you have hoped and prayed for a very long time.

18

She is coming back to us bit by bit. An eyelid lifts, a pupil drifts like a tiny chunk of ice floe, a murmur barely crosses the frontier of her lips, then she sinks back into limbo. All she does is ripple the surface like a whale coming up for air.

* * *

She has uttered her first coherent words, but there's something wrong. She kept asking for a mysterious individual called Grelot. Grandmother explained to me this was a Persian cat, a family pet when Mama was a little girl. It died twenty years ago. Misled no doubt by the decoration of her childhood room, she is coming back to life in the shrunken shape of a kid who has lost her way, and it worries her to find her parents so changed, so much older all of a sudden. As for me, she doesn't recognize me at all. That's only natural since I belong to a distant, inconceivable future.

She is now calling for her older brother, Hugues, and still clamouring for her pussy cat. Dr. Lacroix, whom Grandmother telephoned, advises us to wait; he feels we should avoid at all costs giving her a shock. He says this sojourn in the past is most likely just a stopover on the road that will take her back to us. I hope so, because I can't imagine myself bringing up my own mother.

* * *

This morning, the tape of Mama's memory kicked in at the right spot. She called me by my name, and all her years had caught up with her. But our joy was short-lived, because now we had to answer her questions about the room, about that impossible August scene at the window, about the immense weakness that was weighing her down. The last thing she could recall dated back to February — the promise of an exciting snowmobile ride. But of the outing itself she remembered nothing. She wanted to see Papa and grew uneasy when we didn't respond. Grandfather took it upon himself to tell her about the fifty-fourth kilometre. He chose his words with the utmost care, but the truth proved to be too grim and, my heart slowly breaking, I watched a telluric horror cracking my mother's face inch by inch. Her only reaction was an ominous, bloodless silence. I would have much rather that she'd wept or screamed, but I saw a monumental lassitude descend upon her. Her gaze closed up. Her hand froze in mine. I thought I heard the blizzard moaning behind the walls. Kilometre 54 took advantage of her extreme vulnerability to

119

recapture her, and this time Papa had nothing to do with it.

She has been ice-cold to the touch ever since. Dr. Lacroix tells us to be patient yet again, but what does he know about the evil spells of the vast immaculate dream? What if Mama was being swept away for good this time? Luc refuses to let the miracle come to nothing. He talks about carrying Mama into the cave so she'll be able to soak up the iguana's regenerative emanations. Better still, he suggests we smuggle the lizard into the house and hide it under the bed or in the cupboard in order to bring them as close together as possible. Another crackpot scheme of his. After supper we'll head out to the Cove to ask for advice and pray, even though our hearts aren't in it. I can already guess what I'll be dreaming about tonight: a cold-storage place where Mama will lie slumbering like Snow White in a matrix of ice, with Luc and me, resembling a pair of mournful dwarfs, kneeling by her side.

* * *

In the dead of night, I heard sobbing in Mama's room. When I entered the murky aquarium, I found her fully conscious, floating alone in the darkness. She was weeping over her misfortune, and since it was mine as well, we mingled our tears. My mother's bed was a flimsy raft riding a heaving sea of sorrow. More than once I thought we would capsize, but we drifted on and on until we landed on the luminous shores of dawn. Mama has fallen asleep again but remains warm to the touch. I don't know anymore how to thank the iguana. I would need to coin new words of praise, compliments no one has ever heard before.

* * *

It still happens that Mama suddenly nods off, but it's an ordinary kind of sleep from which she is easily roused. This time, she is really back, but all those months of inertia have sapped her strength. Regaining it will be a long process. She'll have to fight to take possession of her body again, and I'll struggle along with her. I'll be her scout on the road to recovery. I'll beat a beautiful, wide trail for her with the snowshoes of my optimism. The Local Centre for Community Services will fly in a physiotherapist twice a week, and I'm going to study his techniques, for I plan on becoming Mama's discipline and exercise guru. I'll be her gentle trainer, her great big walking smile.

* * *

Mama is working hard. She is doing her best, but it's difficult. Right now, she can barely lift a spoon. I make an aerobic show of confidence and applaud even her tiniest effort. I massage her poor, sore muscles while I babble on about anything that pops into my head to outwit her grief and dispel her gloom. I fill the gap in her memory by reciting all that has happened these past months. Naturally, we talk about Papa, although we dare not plumb the shaft his death has bored in our lives. Mama confided to me she often dreams about a golden mask bending over her. I would like to help her understand but think it wiser to wait until her body is stronger and her heart has mended. At that time, I mean to tell her everything. Besides, having to explain Luc's presence is quite enough for now.

Mama wanted to know who that shaggy-haired boy was who kept walking past her bedroom but never came in. I made the introductions while Luc stood rooted to the doorstep, looking like a squid in a pot of chowder. Too shy to string three words together, he bolted, and we haven't seen him since. To justify this odd behaviour, I told Mama all the good things about my friend. She was touched when she heard he didn't have a mother anymore. And once I revealed Luc had been a great support to me during the time I was an orphan, she was overcome with gratitude. She would like to thank him, but he has vanished. Gone into hiding at the Cove, I guess.

* * *

Mama is trying to win Luc over. She greets him whenever he walks by and emphasizes each one of her overtures with a smile, but he proves to be difficult to tame. The problem is that my mother is a supernatural being in his eyes, a kind of angel who dazzles him, and he'd rather worship from afar. He doesn't dare go near her. He is afraid to disturb Mama or be an eyesore to her. But he still brings mystical pebbles and jars with coloured sand which he asks me to set down at her bedside. These presents must be invested with magical healing powers, for they have a soothing effect on Mama. They seem to lessen her sorrow, and she is able to talk more calmly then about Papa. So Luc is helping in his own way to lighten her mourning...

19

The days are getting shorter, the nights chillier. The sky is turning dark and leaden over the heads of us flabbergasted kids. We resign ourselves, for autumn is upon us with its treacherous weather and angry moods, its sheets of rain and monochrome hours. It's time for old movies and chips in the afternoon, and marathon games of Monopoly while raindrops patter away on the roof. We go back to school tomorrow. A gloomy event. Luc and I will be going to a new place because secondary school's welcoming tentacles are reaching out to us. We'll be attending the high school in Villeneuve. We have no choice, apparently. This is how it is and that's that.

* * *

Every morning and afternoon we take Pollux's yellow bus. He's an ex-hippie who always has good rock playing while we're on the road. Villeneuve High is kind of a huge fallout shelter where two thousand students shut themselves up at set times to gather knowledge, migrating in herds at the sound of a bell. *I* may be able to get used to it, I think, but Luc is panicking. Wild-eyed, he studies his timetable and systematically heads for the wrong classroom. In the corridors, he moves against the stream of traffic and constantly bumps into people. How he misses his radiator at the back of the one-room schoolhouse! And that good old window looking out over the sea! His eyes used to be glued to it. Here, the windows are few, narrow, and show only other dreary scenes. Having been suckled by the open air and cradled by the surf, Luc instinctively hates this concrete, these neon lights, this crowding. He is utterly miserable. Whenever he can, he rushes off to shut himself up in his locker, a kind of vertical coffin where he mutters away in merman jargon. It's quite a challenge to get him to come out. Already, he has started to cross off the days on his schedule. The school year will be long.

* * *

This going-back-to-school business is a bad deal. The worst inconvenience is the lack of time. The attention devoted to Mama has diminished greatly as a result. As for opportunities to slip away to the Cove, they've dwindled down to a precious few. We're only able to go and salute the iguana on Saturdays. My faith is suffering because of it. Now that the sacred odour surrounding the miracle has faded, reason is doing its best to get the upper hand. I occasionally wonder if magic did in fact occur or whether I simply imagined it all. But as soon as I see the old lizard, my doubt vanishes. The iguana has that way of hypnotizing you. I always want to touch him to remember what it's like. I'll stroke his geological crest, his grungy-dragon tail, his dark claws, anxious to experience those pins and needles in my fingertips again, that electrical tingling that's like a mild current from a battery.

* * *

The saurian forgives us our slackness and keeps supplying me with fresh dreams. He lets me glimpse luminous lagoons under Polynesian night skies, and round, wild bird's eyes fixed on me as though I were a worm that had lost its way. Suddenly I spot an island, a cliff lashed by the waves. I dive deep below the surface of the water, boldly glide over steep slopes, peer down at thrilling undersea vistas. These are novel, inexplicable dreams, invaded more and more by the sea. Am I on the verge of turning into a merman, too? Is the iguana sending echoes of homesick longing for his native islands into my soul, or is it my friend, rather, who is influencing me? It may be the overflow of Luc's night visions spilling into mine. Because his dreaming has reached oceanic proportions since we went back to school. His swims are frenzied, his wanderings fantastic. On the back of powerful manta rays, Fngl soars over peaks of briny mountains and he clashes in single combat with protoplasmic entities. He pursues the

Shimmering City into the depths of abyssal canyons, and every once in a while, at the end of a dream, as he scans the watery distance, he catches sight of the violet halo cast by the town's lights. Then the drifting city seems close by. The fish swirl in its wake, the waves still resonate with the conchs' fading hum, and Fngl knows he is almost there, he'll set eyes on the tendrilled town soon. Luc, too, now only lives for this. His search for beautiful Ftan has become urgent, more vital than ever since we went back to school. I even think he needs it for his mental health. Dreaming has always been a natural release for Luc, a way to skirt around the horrors of reality, but nothing he has lived through until now can compare with the daily torments of Villeneuve High. He sees it as the exact opposite of Ftan, the nightmarish counterpart of the glorious underwater realm. Slipping back every night into his merman skin is becoming like a drug, a pain reliever he requires in increasingly massive doses, just to keep going.

* * *

Any excuse will do to flee the hated school. Instead of going to classes, Luc escapes and, like a fool, I follow him into town. Luckily, Grandfather has asked me to sort the post-office mail for him. Now I'll be able to intercept my non-attendance reports and dodge reprimands. Luc has no worries on that score because the Pig tosses letters from school straight into the garbage can, along with all his bills, without even opening them.

We treat ourselves to terrific extracurricular escapades. We start off at the amusement arcade, but Luc will instinctively head for the sea, and before long we're at the harbour, mingling with sailors out on a spree who are swarming the neighbourhood. As we amble along, we love to overhear their shouts in Greek or Italian, their inflections from Portugal or Japan. At the corner of Maltais Street is The Beluga, a shop where they sell diving gear. Luc winces as he studies the outrageous prices of the diving suits. So that he'll feel better, we go and haunt the docks. We sniff the heady smells of iodine and fresh iron, of engine oil, of fish, of sidereal horizons. We roam the quays, explore the hangars. But most of all we marvel at the ships. Standing on guano-soiled bollards, we gauge the tonnage of anchored freighters, sing out their exotic names. Then we saunter over to the Vieux Quai to watch a returning shrimp boat or a weary crabber. Or we'll lean over the shoulder of a fisherman to peer into the lustrous, bronze depths and catch the viridescent ballet of rocklets and smelts. Out of the goodness of our hearts we toss back into the water the stupid anglerfish that keep swallowing the bait meant for nobler finny creatures.

20

Autumn reveals its colours while Mama is regaining hers. We've rented a wheelchair and I push her around, watched enviously by Luc, but she doesn't really want to go anywhere. Most of the time she'll ask me to station her at the window and she'll read poems by Supervielle, by Nelligan. Or just sit there gazing out, as though looking at a distant, fantastic landscape, no longer within her reach.

* * *

She felt stronger this morning and, after breakfast, she asked to see my father's grave. First I dashed up the hill to make sure no trace of our digging remained, then I wheeled Mama over. We lingered for a long while in the bare cemetery, conversing only in our minds amid the whirling leaves. My father's eye winked in the low-hanging sun that gilded our brows. His presence could be felt in sovereign autumn's every manifestation, yet Mama didn't notice a thing. Papa's death appears to be taking up permanent residence within her. The problem is no longer the physical aspect of her recovery but its mental dimension: it is her soul that is slow to heal. How can we throw off this shroud wrapped around her heart?

* * *

Luc is smartening up. He has set himself the task of taking Mama's mind off her worries. That buffoon of the beaches has decided to make her laugh, so each time he walks into her room he is decked out in some disguise. He'll put a lampshade on his head, or a salad bowl. He'll fashion elephant ears for himself with his socks and try to mimic all the crazy characters he sees on TV. He'd like to be Luc the clown, the Master Gagman, but he's actually quite pitiful and deserves his nickname 'the Mongolian' more than ever. But the big surprise is that Mama smiles at his antics. Sometimes she'll even laugh out loud, which is music to our ears. She is simply being kind to him, of course, since he's just a poor motherless boy. Mama knows he's trying to quench his thirst for a mother's love through her and she goes along with it. She's agreeing to stand in for the female lead in Luc's play who disappeared during the first act.

* * *

She calls him her little clown, and I always find him hanging around her room, prostrating himself, bending over backwards a hundred and eighty degrees. He says he wants to anticipate her every need, but that's just a pretext to stay close to her and worship her to his heart's content. He sketches fish, asterias, seaweed, mermaids for her. Mama is dazzled by his talent, and I must confess that jealousy knots my guts, since I can't draw worth beans. Their relationship is taking on a closeness that upsets me, but I'm unable to hold it against them. Hasn't Luc earned the right to share my mother a bit, seeing that he contributed so much to her rebirth? Besides, he really does draw well. He can't be blamed for that, can he? And anyway, their chats remain perfectly innocent.

* * *

He has sketched a portrait of Chantal for Mama and peppered her with questions. This mad notion, this fabricated nostalgia just won't let go of him. It seems to be buried, yet it's always there, just below the surface of his soul, waiting for an opportunity to emerge. Mama had to disappoint him. She never knew his mother because she wasn't even living in the village at the time of Chantal's death; she was away at university. Chantal's lovely face is therefore unfamiliar to her, but she asked Luc if he had any other relatives on his mother's side. Uncles, cousins, grandparents? Luc doesn't know. His father has never mentioned anyone and, obviously, Luc never asked. But when Mama offered to question the Pig on his behalf, he quickly refused. She insisted, because she thinks it's important that we find out, and Luc promised to attend to it that very evening. A narrow escape for the poor guy. The mere thought that Mama's purity might be sullied by coming into contact — even by phone — with the Pig's visceral coarseness makes him sick.

* * *

I guess the Pig didn't much care for his son's questions, since Luc turned up this morning with a cut lip. He claimed it was the result of a bad fall, but no one believed his story. Shaking with righteous anger, Mama picked up the telephone to call Children's Aid, but Luc begged her not to. He told her about his morbid fear of being carted off to a foster home. Mama gave in but demanded to be wheeled over to the Pig's place so she could at least give him a piece of her mind. Grandfather objected. He decided that he himself would go and beard the fisherman in his den. He put on his cap and strode off in a manly fashion. Luc was in a cold sweat, but relaxed an hour later when Grandfather returned alive and well, although deathly pale, and minus his cap. Refusing to comment on his visit to the Pig, he closeted himself with Grandmother in Mama's room, and they held one of those detestable confabs reserved for adults. Ten minutes later, they called us in. They will respect Luc's wishes. They won't notify Children's Aid, but forbid my friend to ever set foot in his father's place again. From now on, he'll live with us. Luc is all for it. Choking back tears, he blurted out his thanks and swore to be worthy of our trust. So here I am, with a brand-new adoptive brother! The five of us will form a new-style family — a crazy quilt, to be sure, but with the heart of a lion. Just let the Pig dare come for his son and watch what happens!

21

Grandmother has taken hold of Luc and enrolled him in a rigorous personal-hygiene instruction programme. It's conditioned-reflex training that intensifies at the approach of mealtimes and culminates at night in major scrubbings. Luc means business. He is even beginning to smell good. Pavlov would be proud of him. Grandmother rewards Luc by showering him with small, practical gifts such as toothbrushes, nail-clippers, and pajamas, and he responds to this generosity by treating her with boundless respect. He agrees to take on the civilized veneer Grandmother imposes on him and does his best to fulfill her lofty ambitions. He is willing to satisfy her on all counts but one: we'll have to forget about him getting rid of his old cap and Newfie boots. As ratty as these articles may be, they are his personal insignia, something Grandmother will simply have to put up with. She has given in and tries to ignore these items. Now that she's abandoning the idea of improving Luc's extremities, she is concentrating on the middle section and, already, has nothing but praise for him. Actually, to listen to her, he'll soon be sprouting wings, and a halo will blaze around his head: scratching Luc's surface and marvelling at what she brings to light, she assigns all kinds of imaginary qualities to him. He is becoming a paragon of virtue in her eyes. Poor Grandmother. Luc — civilized? If she could only see him at the Cove doing a voodoo dance in his Stanfields while yelping like one possessed to invoke the avenging elements each time the Pig puts out to sea!

* * *

The mystery surrounding Luc's family remains unsolved, but Mama is tackling it with the zeal of a first-rate detective. It's giving her something to do, something important to accomplish, another reason for living, actually. She sent us off to the presbytery to get Luc's baptismal certificate. Flipping through the register between two mouthfuls of tart, Father Loiselle produced a copy of the document, and Luc studied it with eager interest, because this was the first time he laid eyes on such absolute proof of his existence. Listed on the page were his parents' places of birth. As a bonus, so were the dates. Chantal Bouchard was born in Rimouski. She was twenty-eight last month. She would have been.

Now we have the name of a town, we've got a lead. If Luc has any relatives, that's where we may be able to find them. With Mama, we went over the Bas-Saint-Laurent telephone directory with a fine-toothed comb and made an inventory of two hundred and six Bouchards spelled various ways. Among them were twelve Chantals. The next stage will be to phone all these people.

* * *

We've turned Mama's bedroom into a mini-telephone exchange and are calling across the Gulf. We can reasonably expect to unearth some of Luc's relatives, and this prospect whets his imagination, but not as much as one might think. He goes along with the tracking down of relatives, should there be any, but couldn't care less really about getting to know these strangers. What interests him in Mama's project is the possibility of questioning the twelve Chantals. He hopes to find his mother this way — not the mermaid, but the real one, the two-footed mother — and that fires him up. He stubbornly persists in talking about her as though she were a living person, and if I happen to make the big mistake of voicing even the semblance of a doubt, he immediately hops on his high seahorse to defend the theory of her being alive. He maintains she simply staged the drowning to cover up her flight. He thinks she may have decided to go back to live on the south shore, and he is so sure of this that I've ended up sharing his belief. It's not impossible, after all.

* * *

We've completed our telephone survey. We've exhausted the list of Bouchards and, from start to finish, they swear they've never heard of Luc. As for the Chantals, not one of them wanted to acknowledge she was his mother. Anyway, there is no proof that she returned to her native haunts. She may just as well be in Tokyo, for all we know. Or be living somewhere under a different name. Luc thinks we mustn't rule out the possibility that one of the Chantals may have lied, but how should we go about clearing that up? Make them all take a lie detector test? Luc would like to question them in person. He feels he would be able to see into their hearts. If it were up to him, he'd be on the next bus to Rimouski.

* * *

He has disappeared. We've seen neither hide nor hair of him since yesterday and everybody is uptight. I went to check the spot where he hides his loot and found the tire empty. The list of the Bouchards is missing, too. He has obviously gone to Rimouski. The son of a gun just couldn't resist.

* * *

He called from a phone booth a minute ago and apologized for worrying us. I heaped reproaches on that nutty caveman, but he said he had no choice, we would never have let him go off on his own. He is not wasting his time in any case: he's scouring Rimouski, knocking on doors and interviewing candidates. He has already eliminated nine Chantals. There are three left for him to see. He promised to come back tomorrow.

* * *

We went to pick him up at the bus terminal. I suspect he hasn't eaten in three days. He is coming home empty-handed, convinced at last that none of the Chantals is the right one. My mother had a serious talk with him about things one simply doesn't do. I think he understood. He won't let himself get quite so carried away again.

He seems subdued and acts the sensible guy, but that's only a façade. His heart and soul are still in a turmoil. He smells the wind, hunting for a new lead. He is still quite sure that his mother is alive and must have left some traces along the way. There must be *some*one out there who knows, he insists. Besides the Pig, of course, who doesn't count, because we'd probably need to torture him to make him talk, and giving that a shot doesn't appeal to us in the least. How about the neighbours? Since Luc is incapable of getting them to confide in him, I offered to take care of that.

* * *

The Trépaniers, on the west side, filled me with pudding but became tight-lipped when I brought up the subject of Luc's mother and stated they didn't know anything about her. I was even less successful on the east side, at Monsieur Cormier's place: at the mere mention of the name Bezeau, the fellow became irate and threw me out. I tried my luck at the Desrosiers' as well, then at the Keenes', but at both places I came up against a wall of silence. They all claim they don't know. They pretend they haven't a clue. It reeks of dishonesty and confirms Luc's suspicions, but meanwhile the ghost of the lovely Chantal remains as elusive as ever. Luc feels intensely blue. He's still positive she is walking the earth somewhere and he'd give anything to know where that might be. We still have the iguana, though, with its serene smile and coralline dreams which my sluggish brain fails to penetrate. Luc has lain a portrait of his mother on the altar and is waiting for an idea, a dream. Who is she? Where can she be? And where, I wonder, is Luc himself when, standing in front of the mirror, he studies his features until his eyeballs are about to pop out while he mumbles away in the language of Ftan? It's as though he was expecting some kind of revelation from these sessions of self-hypnosis. Is he hoping his reflection might come to life and tell him where his mother is hiding? 'Mirror, mirror, on the wall...'

22

The promise of an early winter made me fear a possible relapse. I was afraid the chill might remind Mama of other — painfully recent — cold seasons. But I'm reassured, for she doesn't appear to be disturbed by the mercury's drop. She actually seems invigorated by it: the wheelchair isn't used anymore except for our Grand Prix races and other ballistic experiences. Now that she's steady on her legs, Mama paces up and down the hard, sandy beach every day, and her strides are getting longer, her cheeks ruddier in the strong, bleak wind gusting in from Labrador. She stubbornly insists on going out bareheaded, without gloves or a scarf. She has hot flashes, and Grandmother follows her around in the house with a shawl, turning up thermostats, closing windows that Mama leaves wide open wherever she goes. By the look of it, her icy stay at Kilometre 54 has rendered her immune in a way.

* * *

The potholes frosted over, then the first snowfalls buried us. This was all Grandfather was waiting for; his snow blower stood at the ready, primed right up to its mouth. But Luc offered to clear everything with a shovel, including the driveway. He explained it was his job at the Pig's and had become a habit, a kind of winter sport he enjoyed. Since it seemed to matter so much to him, Grandfather agreed. He'll keep his snow blower for special occasions, for real blizzards.

* * *

Luc wasn't joking. When I came downstairs this morning for breakfast, that scruffy yeti was already outside, happily slaving away. Since the driveway is thirty metres long and was covered with a thick white blanket, I felt obliged to go and give him a hand. I teamed my shovel with his, and together we swiftly wrapped it up. But lo and behold! tonight it's snowing again, and I'm beginning to regret being so helpful this morning. Have I created a dangerous precedent, I wonder?

* * *

The pirouetting flakes are making Mama edgy. With Ski-doo fever, that Nordic malaria, spreading through her as it does every year, she is raring to go, but it's quite out of the question we would ever let her climb on one of those blasted contraptions again. To take her mind off it, I suggested we get out our skates instead, and we went to cut the ice at the school after supper. Dodging Lilliputian astronauts and puck pushers, we whirled around under the floodlights like Olympic clowns and waltzed to tinny music while Luc stood chomping at the bit behind the sideline. He doesn't know how to skate and deeply distrusts this shady activity. He followed us up and down the rink, eyeing my mother anxiously, afraid, I'm sure, that she might take a tumble on that slippery surface and break into a thousand pieces like a fragile figurine.

* * *

Despite the pall cast by my father's absence, all augurs well for the holidays. Luc is lending a hand with the decorating and even the cooking, offering to act as Grandmother's kitchen boy while she makes her tourtières. As nimble as a chimpanzee, he scaled the verandah to festoon the house with brilliantly coloured lights. He also helped put up the Christmas tree, on the boughs of which he hung sparkling balls, along with a few mackerel bones for an even prettier effect.

* * *

Clearing the driveway has become an early-morning ritual, a kind of muscular reflex. It's quite a pleasant routine, really, and gives us a chance to compete in some wonderful, virile contests. High on endorphins, we'll forge ahead from both ends of the driveway and quickly dispatch the snowdrifts as we aim for the hockey stick that serves as a flag at the centre, while Grandfather holds his stopwatch and cheers us on. At other times, when we're in an artistic mood, we take the trouble to carve big, beautiful, pristine blocks out of the wintry expanse, which we leave in the middle of the road as our signature.

* * *

Our Christmas Eve party was loads of fun. Grandfather got a wind gauge and Grandmother a new sewing machine. Mama plugged her new iPod into the speakers and played Christmas carols while I feverishly unpacked my computer. For Luc, I'd bought real, top-quality flippers and, following my suggestion, my grandfolks gave him a diving mask. Grandmother also presented him with an amazing pair of corduroy pants. To each of us he gave a gift he'd cobbled together in his workshop at the Cove. For me, he'd made a chain from crab claws — a symbol of the pact that unites us and a token of our friendship. For Grandfather, he had chiselled a most impressive ashtray out of a whale vertebra, and he gave Grandmother a lovely little mirror framed with plaited rushes. My mother's present had been his biggest worry for the past few weeks. Since he couldn't think of anything that would be beautiful enough for her, he'd procrastinated until the very last minute and then hastily crafted a pair of delicate ear pendants set with tiny seashells. Mama likes them a lot. Her gift to him was an art supply kit, made up of canvases, oils, charcoal sticks and inks, but she had another present for him as well: she'd bought him skates. Although completely baffled at first, he hurried over to the rink this morning to christen them, learning under my supervision. He covered more distance on his backside than on the blades, and there were times when he turned into an uncontrollable missile only the sideline could stop, but I know he won't give up, bruises or no bruises; he has made up his mind he'll master this new means of transport and he *will*, no matter what, for it's a question of honouring my mother's gift.

Since we didn't want the iguana to be left out of the general rejoicing, we put on our snowshoes and headed out to the Cove to throw a small Christmas Eve party just for him. After placing a red hat on his flat head and draping his crest with tinsel, we sang a few Christmas tunes, then I laid a panoramic photo of the Galápagos Islands in front of him, which I'd swiped from a *National Geographic*. Throughout the celebration, the lizard only gave us his ever-present Mesozoic smile, but I could tell he was enjoying himself.

* * *

Winter won't stop us from paying our respects to the iguana. In spite of the deep snow, we continue to crisscross the Gigots and often visit that icebox where the iguana hibernates. Actually, as soon as we light a fire, the cave becomes quite comfortable — cosy enough, at least, for us to take off our parkas and work on Luc's fresco. I help him doing the seabed and occasionally furtively scrawl a tiny merman in some corner or other, while right against the vault, just outside the alcove, Luc paints away like a third-rate Michelangelo. He is trying to portray the octopus-headed monster he sometimes meets on the route to Ftan and whom he fights but has never been able to defeat. I don't know if it's intentional, but the monster's eyes conjure up those of the Pig...

23

If a diver fails to follow the dive tables or his ascent rate is too fast, nitrogen bubbles may form in his body. This is called a decompression accident.

We never hear of the Pig anymore. The animal seems to have forgotten Luc exists. We always make long, superstitious detours to avoid the yellow house and won't even utter the name of its loathsome occupant, for fear that the mere vibration of the word may trigger something.

Living among normal people is doing Luc good. A few kilos have been added to his scrawny frame. He is filling out and now combs his hair like a pop singer, but that's only the tip of the iceberg, the visible part of a more profound change. He is undergoing a transformation. You only need to open his sketchbook to understand. Mermaids and other sea creatures turn up less often; they mingle with terrestrial landscapes, caricatures of teachers, drawings of ordinary objects and scenes from everyday life. Even his mother's portrait, which used to be everywhere, now only turns up here and there, while there are plenty of pictures of *us*. I think this is a sign of a favourable development, of a better adjustment to the world. It's as though Luc's ether was condensing, as though the ground under his feet was becoming firmer. By prosaically rubbing shoulders with our little group, he is growing accustomed to reality. He will never give up the realm of dreams — the place where his heart is — but he doesn't pray to the iguana quite as urgently as before. His fantasies still play to a full house every night, yet he no longer curses daybreak. Ftan continues to be his ideal destination, but he is now subjected to the strong pull of a family, a home, and a new gravitational equilibrium is establishing itself. After steering clear of the shores of human society all his life, Luc has found a port to put into at last! This sailor of inner waterways, this lover of the high seas of the imagination, this denizen of the waves who has always preferred the peaceful depths to the turbulent surface, is suddenly taking the risk to emerge. Horrible reality, which he'd only ever perceived through a prism of pain, is beginning to have an unexpected appeal for him; he is discovering you can put down roots in it without sacrificing your dreams, and this is a major revelation. Luc accepts the challenge. He agrees to come out of hiding. Even at school he is trying to get used to things. He no longer takes refuge in his locker and practises walking calmly in the middle of the corridors. Yet he prefers the hermetic quiet of the library, where he spends as much time as possible studying like mad. Since one has to do something useful in life, my friend has decided to become a great deep-sea scientist, a kind of new and improved Cousteau.

* * *

With winter doddering into senility, spring disputes its authority and has begun asserting itself, sculpting the beach, furrowing it with torturous trickles. The Gigots are melting too, which makes our pilgrimages to the Cove easier. We forget our scarves on the hallway bench. Viruses take advantage of this to launch the offensive. Then thermometres are deployed, the handkerchief war begins, ending eventually with the revenge of the corpuscles. There's a rich, pervasive smell of fertile humus in the air, and Mama is sensitive to this phenomenon of universal regeneration. Now that the days are lengthening, Mama is restless. She pores over the newspaper, scans the want ads, studies the job opportunities. She misses her independence, would like to become an adult once again. In private, she talks of moving to town soon, but hesitates on account of the repercussions. It's just that my grandfolks have aged considerably as a result of their recent worries and we are reluctant to turn our backs on them after all they've done. There's also Luc we don't want to leave behind and whom we'd need to talk into coming along to Villeneuve, which won't be easy. Mama foresees a heartrending parting and that stops her from wanting to pull up stakes. She says we need to give it a bit more thought, then once again puts off the final decision. That's fine with me. As far as I'm concerned, there's no hurry.

* * *

With the good weather, all sorts of migratory birds are showing up again, including some of the funnier ones: Joël, Marc, and Luigi, Luc's diver friends. They've wintered in Martinique and have returned golden brown on both sides. They've landed another contract at the port of Villeneuve and have happily moved back into their old mouse hole. The guys have blown a bundle — they've treated themselves to a big Zodiac with a ninety horsepower motor, in which they skim the swells every night after supper. We jump at every invitation to join them; I can't think of anything more exciting than gulping sea spray like this at the speed of sound. Luc likes to sit in the bow and take it all in, but when we roar past the Pig's place, he turns his head away. He doesn't even want to risk catching a glimpse of his poor excuse for a father. Anyway, the beast is nowhere to be seen. Indifferent to the changing seasons, the Pig remains cooped up in his private Sahara, and the rowboat gathers moss on its blocks. Only the occasional absence of the truck attests to the existence of some kind of larval life form.

* * *

The caplins are back and the bottle hunt is on. It promises to be a fruitful season. Luc eagerly haunts the shore, because Joël, who wants to modernize his diving gear, has promised to sell him his breathing regulator and old scuba tanks for peanuts. The beaches are coming to life. Fires leap up again. Grandfather is dusting off his repertoire of tall tales and trotting out new versions of them that are more horrible than ever.

* * *

Suddenly, there's the explosion of summer, its atomic budding, its pyrotechnics of tantalizing promises — and the highlight of these fireworks is that school's out. For a time, which we hope will be elastic, school and all such tedious things can go to the devil as far as we're concerned. We are tight coils of heightened senses. We sleep less so as not to waste anything, for we need to savour every drop of the intoxicating elixir that flows from the sun's casks and fill up our pores with the pure photons it distills. We gorge on freedom. Like nature that's buzzing all around us, we're in a hurry to grow, to live a thrilling existence, a life raised to the zillionth power.

* * *

To top it all off, who should suddenly appear but Uncle Hugues! Hugues, whom we hadn't heard from in two years except for a single postcard mailed from Liberia. Hugues, who showed up out of the blue in the middle of supper, setting down his suitcase, plastered with distant destinations, in the doorway. Hugues, the vagabond, the adventurer, whom my grandfolks welcomed with mixed feelings, since he is the least pristine sheep of the family. Mama and I rushed into his arms, though, for he's her big brother and my very favourite uncle rolled into one.

Hugues and Mama have always belonged to one another. Leaning over the cradle of that baby girl born on his sixth birthday, Hugues decided she was his present, and she has been his most precious possession ever since — his elf, his pocket angel, his treasure. Was she thirsty? He would rush to the store to get her a Pepsi. Did she want a ball? He'd filch one from some child in the neighbourhood. Had she admired ballet shoes on a TV show? He would manage to get her a pair from Quebec City. Did she wish for the moon? He would instantly make up his mind to become an astronaut. There wasn't anything he couldn't get hold of for his princess in felt booties, and this unbridled love was mutual, for she idolized her big brother, that all-powerful magician. No girl ever had a more chivalrous brother or a fiercer protector — nobody would have dared lay a finger on Hugues's little sister. It even became a problem during her teenage years, since he was extremely particular as to her choice of suitors and succeeded in driving them off one by one. Only Papa

151

had found favour in his eyes, perhaps because Papa was so much like himself, and that is actually why I'm so fond of that beanpole Hugues. I worship him not just because he is the most dynamic and irreverent of all my uncles, but because he reminds me of my father. That's the reason I love him so much, now more than ever. That's why I threw myself into his earthy smell and hugged him so tightly I almost dislocated my shoulders.

Between two kisses, Hugues explained he had just flown in from Africa. He had gone straight to our house in Villeneuve and when he found it deserted, he'd inquired at a neighbour's and was told both my parents were dead. After making a horrified dash for Ferland, he was infinitely relieved to discover that Mama, at least, was alive and well. We gave him an account of everything that had happened. This plunged us into deep sadness, especially Mama, who dissolved in his arms. Hugues choked back his own sobs and did his best to console her. Anxious to rekindle her smile and, for a start, dispel the stifling despondency that clung to her, he suddenly decided to take her dancing. Mama wasn't too sure, but Hugues didn't give her a chance to refuse: he simply stated that she needed to go out, take her mind off things, that Villeneuve's discos were waiting for them, and then told her to go and make herself beautiful.

While Mama was getting ready, Hugues answered our questions about Liberia, Sierra Leone, and Angola, three marvellous countries, then he appeared keen to make Luc's acquaintance. I noticed that my friend was intimidated by that thundering giant, so I butted in to explain that he was now part of the family. Hugues didn't show any surprise whatsoever; he shook hands with Luc and welcomed him as if *he* were the one who had just arrived. Mama came down and took our breath away, because she looked ten years younger all of a sudden. She had done her hair, put on makeup, and changed into her loveliest summer dress. I hadn't seen her as radiant as this for a long time. My uncle whisked her out of the house without wasting a moment, helped her into the gleaming convertible he'd rented at the airport, and they tore off into the night while blowing us a flurry of kisses.

It's late. They aren't back yet but I'm not the least bit worried. I really should go to sleep but I can't. Too excited about my uncle showing up. Because Hugues is the kind of guy to whom problems are like water off a puffin's back. With him around, you can be sure there will never be a boring moment. Eyes wide open as I lie here, my spine tingling when I think of the fun that's about to begin, I can hardly wait!

24

Hugues stirs things up and leads us on a giddy round of activities — a joyful hustle and bustle Luc is a part of, because my uncle has taken a shine to my nutty brother. He thinks he's a scream and insists on dragging him along everywhere we go. We're caught up in a frenzy of movie-going and restaurant visits, in a blitz of shopping trips to replenish Mama's wardrobe so it will be worthy of her, in a frantic whirl of drives, swims, and bare-chested baseball games and Frisbee contests. Today, we flew over the taiga and the northern lakes in a rented Beaver. It was thrilling to gaze down on that shield of old rock crisscrossed by rivers and flecked with innumerable lakes. We landed on the water at the Williams Club, outfitters who cater to salmon-fishing enthusiasts. The manager is a friend of Hugues's. We had lunch at his place. Then we flew south again and finally spotted the Atlantic's jagged coastline. Luc hasn't got over his plane ride yet. In body, he is lying on the bed next to mine, but in his head he is still soaring. Quite a change for him from swimming, which is what he usually does in there.

* * *

That mouth organ Hugues plays like a grizzled old

black man from the bayou is caterwauling away in the living-room, and at night by the fire my uncle steals the show from Grandfather with true stories about guerrilla warfare and crawling through swamps infested with crocodiles and giant leeches. The old man's nonsense pales in comparison, and the competition doesn't sit well with him. He cannot forgive that loutish son of his for daring to rival him in his own house and accuses him of cramming our brains with violent balderdash. I've never really asked myself what sort of work Hugues actually does. I know he is a soldier of fortune, a profession my grandfolks consider dishonourable, but I have always naïvely pictured him as a gallant warrior. A kind of knight-errant. A cartoon-film hero. Could it be, though, that the truth is less dazzling? That my uncle is mixed up in shady business? Sometimes I feel like quizzing him, but deep down I'm not sure I want to know. I only hope he's fighting on the side of a just cause.

* * *

Behind the shed, Hugues gives us jiu-jitsu lessons and lets us benefit from his experience with weapons used in hand-to-hand fighting. He's a real pro with blades. He expertly handles all kinds of pointed instruments and, several times in a row, with screwdrivers of various sizes, he's able to hit Canuel bang in the middle of the heart. Grandfather doesn't much care for these martial-arts sessions. He watches us at it with a sullen look on his face and I can tell he is fuming. He predicts all this fooling around with knives will land us in the hospital, but Hugues merely shrugs, and Mama rallies to his defence when the exchange grows heated. Grandfather always backs off in the end — confronted with the alliance between those two, what else can he do but grumble? Luc totally shares my view: he thinks Hugues is a fantastic guy. He'll tag along when he goes jogging and volunteers when it's time to wrestle in the dust. Luc is captivated by Hugues's paternal aura. He even gets jealous if I slip affectionately under my uncle's muscular arm. Luc's nose is out of joint then, and it takes a lot of tickling to get him to brighten up.

* * *

Hugues's vacation is already coming to an end. He says he has mysterious commitments to honour in the Middle East. He'll be leaving in a few days, and we all feel sad at the thought of this except Grandfather, for the two of them have started squabbling. That's another reason why Hugues thinks it better to leave. To end his stay with a flourish, he has rented a sailboat we'll be boarding tomorrow, with Mama, to go on a mini-cruise in the Gulf. I'll take advantage of it to get to know the basics of sailing.

25

We stepped aboard under a cloudy sky and made for the harbour's exit, but hadn't sailed beyond the islands yet when the wind died away. We had to leave the Bay of Villeneuve powered by the auxiliary engine, without a scrap of glory. Later, it rained. Then, around noon, it got foggy. Bewildered, we dropped anchor off Gallix and ate a tourtière Grandmother had made for us. But the wind rose at dusk and the swells are now a metre high. She's pitching like mad. We're all sick as dogs. There's no way we'll be able to sleep. Thank goodness Luc predicts a smooth sea for tomorrow.

* * *

I've learned to steer, hugging the wind, with the spinnaker full to bursting, and we're cutting through the waves like a butter knife. We made it to Cap-aux-Loutres and back in two days. The water rippled over the hull; even the whales couldn't keep up with us. Half-naked, drenched in sunlight, we pretended we were pirates pursuing imaginary galleons. We even moored at the Caouis to bury our treasure, a big pile of African coins Hugues sealed up in a cigar box. This evening, the last night of Hugues's vacation, we'll berth at Île aux Basques, just off Villeneuve's shoreline. That's where we'll put up our tents.

* * *

Île aux Basques, in the bay, is only one nautical mile from Villeneuve. From our bivouac you could see the houses across the water, and after dark it became like a long string of light. We were morose because my uncle was leaving. The grown-ups discussed the future, and Hugues handed Mama a fat cheque as his brotherly contribution to our imminent settling back in town. Luc panicked, but Mama replied she wasn't ready to move yet. She suggested to Hugues that he retire instead, so he could come and live with us in Ferland, and this is when I had my brainstorm: I proposed we buy a house in the village, not too far from my grandfolks' place, where the four of us would go and live together. My idea was well received by one and all since there was something in it for everyone, and Hugues admitted the prospect was tempting. He promised to think about it.

We felt more cheerful now. Considering the right moment had come, Luc presented Hugues with a parting gift, an amulet made from magic vole bones that was supposed to protect him from the dangers awaiting him. Hugues accepted gratefully and asked if he might also keep as a memento one of the portraits Luc drew of my mother and me while we were anchored off Pentecôte during our odyssey.

Luc opened his sketchbook to let him choose. As he turned over those pages filled with our faces as well as fish and seascapes, Hugues paused at a recent sketch of Chantal, which he studied with interest, remarking that the likeness was striking.

When he saw he had both a captive and inquisitive audience in Luc, Hugues admitted that, yes, he'd known his mother. Luc wasn't about to let such an opportunity slip by; now that he'd finally found a direct witness to his prehistory, he urged him to talk. My uncle explained it was really Bezeau he'd been acquainted with — a drinking buddy from the rowdy days when they belonged to the gang of young hell-raisers who hung out at the Horoscope Bar — but that he'd had a chance to speak to Chantal whenever he dropped by to pick up her husband. Gentle, shy Chantal. And so young. Couldn't have been any older than eighteen. She certainly deserved a better man than that big layabout of a husband of hers, for, with all due respect, Bezeau was hopelessly lazy, and she often had to go fishing in his place. Anyway, the job of cleaning the catch would always fall to her. To say nothing of her housekeeping duties in Villeneuve at the Seamen's Centre. A hard-working little woman. Too nice perhaps, too submissive…

Luc wasn't going to let my uncle off the hook quite so easily. He begged him to tell him more about his mother and the circumstances of her disappearance. But Hugues insisted he really knew very little, that he had only ever exchanged small talk with her — the way people do when they meet briefly at the door — for Bezeau was a jealous man, while she was extremely discreet in any case. As for her death, he didn't have any details. All he ever found out was what people told him when he got back from Chiapas two years later — that sad story of her drowning.

Hugues was anxious to change the subject but Luc pressed him to continue, to tell him how his parents got along together. My uncle grew hesitant. This soldier who, I was sure, could confront an enemy tank without batting an eyelid, suddenly dragged his feet. As carefully as if he were picking his way through a minefield, he mentioned that a noticeable change had come over Bezeau during the weeks following Luc's birth. The fisherman had become belligerent, aggressive, and begun hitting the bottle in earnest. A depression of some sort. Did he ever talk about his wife? Hugues admitted he did, that he'd utter incoherent remarks, mostly into his drink. Harsh words, disjointed drunken ramblings Hugues refused to repeat. And since my uncle preferred to keep silent, Luc filled in the blanks, repeating words he'd heard too many times: slut, whore, bastard... We felt terribly sorry for Luc, but he affected a shrewd iguana smile. He walked away and started to pace up and down the shore. Mama joined him, wrapping her arm consolingly around his shoulders.

Hugues had a long face. He probably blamed

himself for having talked too much. And when I told him that Luc thought his mother was still alive, he looked worried. He mumbled something about muck that would have been better left undisturbed, then made me promise to take good care of my friend. Following which, he slipped into his tent.

Once Mama had gone to bed as well, I went to find Luc at the water's edge. He was catapulting pebbles towards the lights of the city, and I began tossing them too, just to see who could throw the furthest. Luc wasn't exactly chatty, but I knew what he was thinking about: the possibility that the Pig might not be his real father. Another man in his mother's life? Other genes than the Pig's abhorrent ones? Another father — some stranger? With whom Chantal had gone to live perhaps?

His gaze was riveted on Villeneuve's horizontal sweep of stars. He threw a stone in the direction of the lit-up structures of the port, and I knew his hidden target was that Seamen's Centre Hugues had mentioned.

* * *

Nothing could have diverted Luc from the burning trail that had just been cut through the jungle of his past. This morning, after Hugues left, we took the bus to Villeneuve and got off beside the big tent on the Vieux Quai, by the bay.

The Seamen's Centre is a white building near the offices of the Port Authority. It's a drop-in centre with a pastoral orientation. On the door, a sign welcomes you in six languages and lists the times of the religious services. Pushing it open, we stepped into a room furnished with old armchairs, vending machines, and a TV where an American quiz show quietly flickered away. The place was deserted. At the far end loomed an altar made of varnished wood, used for mass no doubt, and a corridor, which we entered, that led to three doors. The first one opened into a large space containing two billiard tables and a dartboard, the second into an unoccupied office. From the third one came a clatter of dishes. We stepped into the doorway. It was a kitchen. Bent over a sudsy sink, with her back to us, stood a woman. Luc gave a start. He was white as a sheet and, for one brief moment, I, too, thought it was her… That she'd remained hidden here all those years, chained to her sink, condemned because of some long-ago transgressions to scour dirty plates for ever and ever. Then the woman turned around and the illusion melted away, for she was at least fifty years old and didn't bear the slightest resemblance to Chantal's portrait. She asked us what we were doing there. I explained we were looking for a Chantal Bouchard who'd worked here eleven years ago. But the name didn't ring a bell with that lady; she had only been employed by the Centre for the past six years. She suggested we come back in the

162

late afternoon so we could ask Father Miron, who was in charge. I dragged Luc outside. A big gulp of sea air put him back on track. We decided to wait for Father Miron and, to make the hours zip by a little faster, we went for a stroll along the quays.

When we returned to the Centre three hours later, an Italian crew had descended upon it. The place was full of guys in pea jackets, calling out to one other and playing billiards while waiting to go into town. We cooled our heels for a while outside the office of Father Miron, since he was busy hearing the confession of a sailor. Then, after that fresh cargo of sins had been unloaded, the priest called us in. A kindly man, though visibly overworked. He listened to Luc revealing the reason for our visit, then explained he had only been in charge of the Centre for the last eight years and had never heard of either Chantal Bouchard or Bezeau. Noticing Luc's dejected look, he wanted to know why he was trying to trace this woman. When he found out she was his mother, he volunteered to get in touch with his predecessor who would probably be able to help us. His name was Father Loiselle. Yes indeed, from the parish of Ferland. Miron wanted to phone him right away, but Luc turned down the offer.

Two real zombies on the bus ride home. Father Loiselle, that life-long ally, that loyal man, that supposed friend of Luc's... Why had he never mentioned the Seamen's Centre? That ambiguous attitude he'd always had towards Luc, at once friendly and uneasy, those small thoughtful gestures, the interest he showed in Luc's health, his well-being... And that fierce hatred the Pig bore him...

The muck Hugues had talked about. A swamp giving off noxious miasmas. The distinct image of a slimy, unhealthy bubble rising to the surface, ready to burst.

26

Decompression accidents can have various characteristics. When nitrogen bubbles lodge in the tissues and joints, cutaneous manifestations may occur (itchiness, rashes, swelling), as well as crippling joint pains, called 'bends,' which appear after the return ascent and diminish twenty-four to forty-eight hours later.

Luc's finger shook when, at twilight, he rang at the presbytery's door. The fat traitor opened up. One look at our funereal faces was enough to make him realize we hadn't come to stuff ourselves, so he led us right into his living-room, a drab parlour saturated with mystical scents, made even gloomier by a large crucifix and the heads of an assortment of popes. We lowered our backsides onto an old velvet sofa. Settling his own bulk comfortably into a matching armchair, the priest inquired after the purpose of our visit. Luc was in no mood for polite chitchat and, coming straight to the point, demanded to be told where his mother was. Loiselle pretended he didn't understand, but Luc fired his first torpedo. He accused him of having lied to him from the very beginning and declared that he now knew the truth — he knew that the priest was his real father.

The portly man turned scarlet. He retorted with a loud 'Oh come now! Of course not!' and similar indignant utterings. The priest sounded genuine and wanted to know where Luc had got such an idea.

'At the Seamen's Centre,' my friend replied, and this time Loiselle really listed to starboard.

It's not easy for a confessor to find himself suddenly on the other side of the sifter of sins. A much less snug position to be in, isn't it? What was he going to do: act stupid, or insult us by denying the accusation once again?

We had carefully worked out a strategy to loosen his tongue and were waiting for a chance to catch the big lump out in a lie, but he chose to make a confession or, rather, offer his apologies. Repentant, contrite, he admitted he had concealed the truth but asked Luc to please believe he had done so for his own good, so as not to disturb his peace of mind, fully intending to reveal everything at a later date, when he'd be old enough. And he went on to expound on the moral obligation to hide occasionally certain truths that are too harrowing. He gradually became his old confident self again and the whole thing turned into a sermon. He trotted out his Sunday voice — his calming, convincing voice — but Luc brought this fine speech to an abrupt conclusion: if Loiselle wasn't his real father, then who was? The priest pulled out a handkerchief and wiped his temples, gazing up at the ceiling as if to call for help from above. Having recovered his serenity to some degree, he held forth at great length about responsibility, duty, and other nonsense suited to the occasion. He was trying to get Luc to believe that it was preferable not to know, wiser to wait until he was more mature, better able to understand. Obviously, *he* was the one who had a problem getting things through his thick skull. Did he still think he could get rid of us by spouting a few hollow phrases? It was time to increase the pressure. We had a tactical confab, using teeth-clicking code, and decided to implement Applying-the-Screws Plan Number One, which consisted in threatening to spread highly unpleasant rumours of pedophilia about him. But we didn't have to resort to such a course of action: alarmed at our cannibalesque jaw games, Loiselle broke down. He cast one final glance upwards in search of the angelic cavalry that failed to materialize, then, realizing we weren't going to give up, he opened his trap to launch into a story that dated back thirteen years.

He talked about meeting Chantal, who had just married the fisherman Bezeau and had recently arrived in the village, a devout young woman whose confession he heard every Sunday. He had become her spiritual advisor. This is how he'd got wind of the couple's problems: Bezeau's alcoholism, his violent nature, the lack of money. That's why he had offered Chantal work as a housekeeper at the Seamen's Centre. Bezeau had objected at first, but the priest promised to keep a watchful eye on her, and the financial benefits appeased the fisherman's

injured pride. Chantal started her new job. The
priest drove Chantal to the Centre in the morning
and brought her back to the village at the end of
the day. Happy to get away from her four walls, the
young woman carried out her duties with zeal. The
economic situation of the Bezeaus stabilized; the
fisherman's mood seemed to be evening out as well.
A year went by in this fashion. But then there had
been that day, and that unthinkable, incomprehensible, terrifying thing...

One late afternoon, when Loiselle returned to
the Centre after running his errands, he found poor
Chantal in the billiard room. She had been attacked
by sailors who had blindfolded her and then used
her. But she begged the priest not to call the police.
She refused to be taken to the hospital. Above all,
she didn't want her husband to know. And Loiselle
promised not to say anything. They both acted as
though nothing had happened. Chantal showed
extraordinary strength; she seemed to be able to
get over the ordeal, to recover without noticeable
after-effects, and perhaps life would have gone back
to the way it was before, if, a few weeks later, she
hadn't found out that she was pregnant. Shaken,
the young woman went to ask for the priest's moral
support. She was afraid to tell Bezeau the truth, so
she thought she might pretend the child was his,
and Loiselle agreed that, in these exceptional circumstances, one was allowed to break the vow of
honesty binding husband and wife. So they risked it:

Chantal announced to the fisherman that he would soon be a father, and the immense pride Bezeau displayed confirmed their belief they had done the right thing.

This is how Luc was born, and the priest christened him while thanking heaven profusely for supplying such a convenient solution. But these praises turned out to be premature, for, one month later, Chantal came to see him in a state bordering on panic with the news that her husband harboured doubts about the child's legitimacy. It was because of his odd appearance, that peculiar oriental gaze, that dark complexion and pitch-black hair, which surprised the fisherman when he first laid eyes on the child, since they didn't correspond to anything one might see in his own family or his wife's. Bezeau had been casting suspicious looks at the baby, uttering caustic references to those DNA tests one heard so much about these days. Chantal didn't know how much longer she would be able to keep up the pretense, and Loiselle listened to her carefully as she voiced her fears because his mind was beset with similar worries: in spite of all their precautions, rumours about what had happened were going around the port. There seemed to have been witnesses to the rape. The story had leaked out, and the possibility of it reaching the fisherman's ears couldn't be ignored. All this led them to face up to a difficult but inevitable obligation: when Chantal asked Loiselle for guidance, he recommended she tell her husband the truth. She agreed it was the only thing to do, provided she could muster up the strength. Loiselle, determined to support her to the end, offered to take care of it and summoned the fisherman.

The priest no longer needed any prodding. Chalk-white, sweat pouring down his body, he was relieving himself of a heavy burden of silence and the words tumbled out as though swept along by a spring breakup of the soul. He told us how he'd received Bezeau in this very parlour. How he'd cautiously revealed what assaults had resulted in Luc's birth, and, in hopes of arousing the fisherman's pity, described the agonies his mother had endured. The priest thought he had succeeded. That evening, when he accompanied poor, stunned Bezeau to the door, he honestly thought he had made it quite clear to him where his duty lay both as a Christian and as a husband. But he underestimated the fisherman's natural paranoia and, the following day, when Loiselle went to see the couple to give them his spiritual assistance, a completely different man loomed in the doorway. A raging, inebriated man, mad with smashed pride. A violent man who refused to believe his wife was innocent. He accused Chantal of having been a willing participant in the gang rape, of having provoked it, and he even suspected the priest of having taken part in it. He swore he'd been deceived and vowed he wasn't going to be conned like this. Loiselle tried to reason with him, but Bezeau brandished his rifle and chased the man he held responsible for his misfortune out of the house. The priest had to retreat, while Chantal and her baby, both in tears, were left behind. He called the police, then prayed that the fisherman's agitation would abate and, with the passing of time, he might begin to understand, learn to accept what had happened. But the fury continued and things only got worse.

Bezeau was no longer in his right mind. Oblivious to his wife's distress, haunted by the child's strange dark features, he turned into a habitual drunk. He rejected the despicable bastard and demanded he be renamed. The house became a cloister where no one was allowed to enter, where Chantal was held prisoner. Loiselle would take advantage of the rare occasions when the fisherman put out to sea to visit Chantal so he could pray with her and comfort her, but the young woman was wasting away in that stifling atmosphere of confinement and constant accusation. Threats were uttered with regard to the child: Bezeau snarled he was going to wring his neck, and Chantal was even afraid to fall asleep, since he might seize the opportunity to carry out his plan and strangle the baby, this son whom she loved in spite of everything. Loiselle urged her to contact a centre for women who are the victims of domestic violence, encouraged her to leave the fisherman and move into town, but she seemed to think this was impossible, he wouldn't let her, he would retaliate. She felt defeated. First the rape, the pregnancy and motherhood, then fear and sleepless nights — all this had exhausted her and thrown her into a depression from which she was unable to recover. Her ordeal blocked her horizon, prevented her from seeing past the next hour, past immediate survival, beyond the care of the child. And in the end the priest felt paralysed and helpless, too.

One night in July, he found her on his doorstep with the child, distraught, soaked from head to foot. She was swollen and terrified, incapable of telling him what had happened. Loiselle called the police again. They picked the fisherman up and remanded him in custody for twenty-four hours. Luc and his mother stayed overnight at the presbytery, and the priest did his best to shake her out of her lethargy, but her mind was too distracted. She had been crushed by the fisherman's acts of cruelty and had begun to think it was all her fault — that she was solely accountable for her fate and everything that had occurred. She believed she deserved this suffering, and none of the priest's denials were able to enlighten her tortured soul. She had spent the following day praying in church. She appeared resigned when Bezeau showed up in the evening to reclaim his family, and quietly followed him. The next day, the sea had carried her off...

Now, the only sound was the wash of the surf at the window. The priest had fallen silent, and the sea was having the last word, just as it did that night in Luc's distant past, just as it has every single night all over the world. The priest had buried his face in his hands. Luc sat totally still. He was a clenched-fisted statue, a scrawny *Thinker*, eyes shimmed with tears, the rigid embodiment of the ankylosis that had infected us all. Each moment's slender filaments entwined with those of the next. A thickening haze of time drifted along the walls. I felt the urge to explode, but there was this stillness pressing on me as sluggishly as freshly poured concrete, pushing me down into the cracks of the sofa, and there was that overpowering emptiness, that silence worthy of Ancient Egypt flowing like a resin and trapping us in its amber. This seemingly permanent stasis was shattered by the priest as he began to speak once more. He announced he had something to give to Luc. He hauled himself out of his chair and left the room. We heard the stairs protesting, then Loiselle came back down again with a yellowed envelope. He explained he had found it in his mailbox the following day, shortly before Chantal's clothes were discovered on the beach. He had meant to wait until Luc came of age before delivering it to him, but now that he knew...

The envelope, already open, was addressed to Luc. It contained a letter he skimmed through, while the priest, wringing his hands, expressed his compassion and recalled the investigation that had been made and the evidence proving that Bezeau had spent the night in a bar in Villeneuve, which obviously cleared him. The letter slipped from Luc's fingers. His eyes had gone dead. I picked the letter up while Loiselle went on talking all by himself. It was a letter from her. A letter in which she told him she loved him immensely, but also a letter saying goodbye, in which she explained she had no strength left to go on living. She was sorry to abandon him like this and asked him to forgive her. She promised she would watch over him from above, where she would dwell from now on. Luc let out a croak and I felt him going limp beside me. He slumped into my arms like a rag doll. He looked transparent, astral; he was barely breathing. I called out his name and shook him. I wanted to get some sign of alertness from him, but he was nothing but raw despair and all he could do was moan. The priest had thrown himself down on his knees to try to revive him as well, stupidly cutting off his oxygen supply. And as if he weren't being enough of a nuisance already, he chose that particular moment to give in to a fit of self-accusatory lunacy: he implored Luc to speak, to answer, and confessed to having failed in his duty, and he asked him to forgive, to understand. Whimpering like a huge beaten dog, he begged to be absolved and raved on and on, too moronic to notice he was jabbering into the void. I ordered him to stop talking such bullshit and, since he didn't snap to it, I gave him a shove. The priest leapt to his feet, then bolted sputtering from the room. I wasted no time lifting Luc up, because he needed to be taken off somewhere, anywhere at all, just so long as he got out of that bewildering madhouse. In the kitchen, the dishevelled priest was waiting for us with a plate of date squares he wanted Luc to eat so he'd cheer up. I yelled at him to get out of the way and, though I've no idea how, we ended up outside.

I remember the swirling stars and my friend's weight on my shoulder. I walked onto the beach. I set Luc down at the bottom of a dune to give him time to get his breath back and gather his thoughts. The salty air did him good: he was breathing better, he began to move again. He stammered out preposterous things about insolent lighthouse keepers, about foghorns that moaned on and on, and about indignant belugas. After a while he started to cry. A real Niagara. Engulfed, desolate and adrift, his mouth wide open, he called his mother. He looked as though he'd been beamed up to a far-off planet of pain. He kept saying it was impossible, she couldn't be dead. He refused to accept that what he'd so stubbornly believed had been an illusion. The priest's story was only a smoke screen, a pack of lies, of course; as for the letter, it was a forgery written by Loiselle himself to fool him. His mother couldn't possibly have abandoned him and gone off and drowned herself like that. The sea wouldn't have allowed it. And, anyway, she *must* have survived since her body was never found — wasn't that proof enough? And yet he knew. He was hanging on by his fingernails to that business about the corpse the sea had never washed ashore, but it was merely the final spasm of a dying hope, because Luc knew very well that mothers weren't like whales, they didn't necessarily beach themselves when death was near. He knew a mother was a weightless little thing that the tides didn't really have a hold on. He knew she could be summoned by the open sea, never to return, and carried off a long way away, into the depths, where her hair might get tangled up in the wrack and she would come to rest among the anemones.

I was crying too, because tears are contagious and I was shaken by the unfairness of it all. Luc would never see his mother's face or bask in her soft embrace. Never, ever would he drop pretty seashells in her lap, or snuggle up in her warmth, or hear the pearly words only a mother knows how to say. Love was dead. But at least he still had hatred, a throbbing hatred I could feel and put a name to. A hatred of fathers — whether they were real or fake. A hatred for the dirty Pig who had sunk his teeth into love's throat and lay snoring this very minute in the stinking yellow house. A hatred for that unknown sailor who had come from the ends of the earth to violate love with his good-for-nothing friends, then shipped out again not having any idea, not even an inkling, of the consequences. And an even fiercer hatred of a village it was a pleasure to picture going up in flames, of a pack of cowards who had let love wither without stepping in. Hatred was something to hold on to. It could sustain you. It was better than nothing. At least it gave you a reason for living.

Luc's eyes finally dried up and he sat rocking,

robot-like, while the sea, that mother-snatcher, glittered slyly as if nothing had happened. Luc coiled up on the side of the dune, utterly spent. I covered him with my sweater and settled down to keep watch. Soon, I heard the gentle lapping of his merman jargon, and that made me happy because it meant he was swimming with his fellow creatures. Luc had found refuge in the familiar waters of his dreams. I knew that *there* at least he was released from grief. Poor old screwball. Why did he have to find out? How I wished someone had stumbled upon him on the beach one morning, in a Moses basket swept onto the shore by the waves, without any clues about his family! Everything would have been so much simpler. So many tragedies would have been avoided.

The night changed into a different costume. The moon hid its languid face behind a mask of cloud. I meant to take Luc back home, but I must have been more exhausted than I thought, because I zonked out too. I had a weird dream. There was that golfer, the one Luc says he sees on the beach some nights. It was a tall, skinny guy, his head wrapped in darkness. He came from the west and paced up and down the shore with long, even strides, swivelling around like a compass on his spindly wading-bird legs. Every now and then he would stop and, with a driver made of pure light, hit phosphorescent balls he'd send soaring high into the sky, among the stars. His visage remained concealed by a patch of opaque blackness, but his sweeping motion was noble, and the luminescent arcs he drew in space were flawless. Oh, the perfection of that golfer's swing...

I woke up flabbergasted with the rising sun beating down on my face. The night had quietly slipped away, and so had Luc, leaving beside me only the imprint of his body. A sinister premonition took hold of my mind. I started out for the Gigots where I thought I might find him. Trudging along, I envisioned the anxious, sleepless night my mother and my grandfolks must have lived through. Luckily, I didn't need to go by our house — where they'd surely be on the lookout for me — but I couldn't avoid the Pig's place. I was still quite a distance away from it when a commotion among the gulls attracted my attention. They were wheeling around just above the trailer, clogging the sky. They'd go into a dive and swoop down quarrelling onto the shore as though fighting over a few succulent scraps of cod. As I came nearer, I saw what was lashing them into such a frenzy: it was in fact a heap of guts, but they couldn't possibly be those of a cod or even a halibut. They had to be at least the entrails of a shark...

Luc was sleeping in the cave with the iguana under his arm. His eyes were open, yet he was asleep. Spattered with blood that wasn't his own, he lay dreaming and gibbering in the language of Ftan. His knife was still in his hand.

27

Luc's gaze slides past mine without making contact. Something seems broken inside. When he woke up, he went to wash himself in the ocean. He cleansed himself of all that dried blood in the most matter-of-fact way, just as though it had been ordinary dirt. He doesn't want to talk about what happened at the Pig's place. Actually, it's not worth mentioning as far as he's concerned. He already sees it as a minor incident compared to what took place while he was dreaming. Because he went to Ftan.

Luc has reached the Shimmering City. He says it's the result of what he did in the yellow house: there's no doubt the Pig had to die for it to become possible. But the beast has been defeated and the death turns out to be justifiable because Luc was finally able to glide along the swaying avenues of the tendrilled town. He has seen Ftan. He now knows the city is a gigantic medusa, a colossal Portuguese man-of-war to whose tentacles cling like clustered eggs an infinite number of transparent ascidians, serving as the aquatic beings' dwelling places. He has entered Ftan, the living symbiotic city that is fed by mermaids while it protects these sirens in return from the ocean's predators. Ftan, which towers above you like a purplish sky with its mucous monuments and inverted minarets meandering in the currents. Ftan, teeming with anemone gardens, with groves of undulating algae. Luc has seen all these things and does his best to describe them to me, but plodder language doesn't have words that can convey Ftan's liquid, pulsating beauty. I would need to borrow his eyes for the fleeting duration of a dream. Anyway, he himself has visited only a tiny part of the City; he just barely had the time to explore its gelatinous suburbs, because once again the vision ended too soon. But he says his next dream will take him to the throbbing heart of the tendrilled domain, all the way to the luxuriant centre where mermen gather. Meanwhile, however, the sun is trying his patience. Luc would like to zap it, fast-forward it. He curses this wheezy day as it creeps along in the Cove. He implores it to give way to the exuberant night and the shifting boulevards of the spellbinding city of sea nymphs.

I don't know what to make of it all. I listen to Luc as he tries to depict every detail of his marvellous vision, but I can't get the scarlet image of the disembowelled Pig out of my mind. How long before the body is discovered and people find out, I wonder? Should I talk my friend into giving himself up or persuade him to make a run for it? Would it be better perhaps to hide the corpse, bury it somewhere, and erase all the traces? In any case, Luc won't listen to me. He's not concerned. He states he won't leave his hideaway at the Cove ever again. He will live here from now on with the iguana to keep him company and with me, whenever I feel like coming to see him. He says he has the waterfall to quench his thirst and the ocean for all the rest, he won't need anything else, he'll be happy here, he'll be able to paint, to dream, and live with complete freedom the solitary existence he loves so much. Poor Luc. He thinks he's safe at the Cove. He imagines people will forget about him after a while, that he'll elude the search and escape into a timeless world, but he's obviously fooling himself. Yet he knows the police have dogs capable of picking up the scent of an oddball hiding out in the deepest reaches of the Gigots, that they have boats, helicopters, and whatever it takes to find someone, but he couldn't care less. Whether the Pig's carcass rots away among the parts of his blasted motor or the police come to get him is all the same to him. From now on, he will live solely to dream and to return to Ftan. Nothing else matters anymore.

Reality is no longer Luc's problem, but it's still very much mine, and more so every minute because we haven't set foot in the house for a whole day now. I'm sure Mama is giving me a good tongue-lashing in her thoughts and I really can't let her fret any longer. I have to go home. But I wonder what reason I should give for Luc's absence. They'll quiz me and I'll have to say something. How can I explain to them that my friend has decorated the beach with his fake father's guts, and thinks he's a fish?

* * *

I was greeted tensely by three grim faces and found myself before a real family tribunal. I was charged with attempting to worry the whole household to death. They demanded to know where Luc and I had spent the night and, first of all, where my accomplice might be hiding instead of appearing before this court. I was at a loss to reply because of the oath of secrecy regarding the Cove's mysteries, so I invented some clumsy story about suddenly deciding to camp out, but it didn't take me long to see I was only making matters worse. They threatened to keep me locked up in my room until I came clean. I knew I'd never be able to keep up the lying, so I made up my mind to confide in my mother and told her in private what had happened. I would have given anything to spare her the horror of that confession, but it was impossible to phrase things delicately, and the shock was brutal. I described Luc's anguished mental state to Mama and struggled to convince her it was urgent for me to go and join him so I could look after him, but she was too shaken. She said she needed time to think and sent me off to bed.

It's dark now and I can't stop wondering about Luc. What is he up to all by himself at the Cove? Is he brooding over my not being back yet? Does he believe I've abandoned him? But perhaps I worry for nothing — he's probably sound asleep already, dreaming like a happy little tadpole about the Great Medusa.

28

Mama came to see me very early to let me know what she'd decided: she was giving me twenty-four hours to bring Luc back. After that, she would notify the police. But I promised that wouldn't be necessary because I was going to bring him home, even if I had to tie him up in a sack. With the help of my grandfolks, who knew nothing but imagined the worst, Mama packed a bag with food for me. Then, on the verandah, she gave me some last-minute advice, made me swear I wouldn't do anything foolish, and instructed me as well to pass on a message to her little clown: she wanted him to remember we all loved him dearly, and to please hurry home. After smothering me with kisses, she let me go, as worried-looking as if I was heading out on an expedition to some distant, unexplored land.

I was determined to force Luc out of his shell. Now that I'd had time to think things over, I was convinced the authorities wouldn't be so cruel as to throw my friend in jail. They'd be moved when they heard his pitiful story and show leniency. They might even commit him to our care, which would be the best solution, of course. I kept rehearsing my arguments as I made my way through the Gigots, and felt quite confident I'd be able to reason with my friend, but as soon as I got there, I saw it wasn't going to be as simple as that, because there was a wacky wind blowing over the Cove. Luc was feverish, elated. He was hopping about like a cricket while he waited for me, desperately anxious to tell me he had finally found his mother.

He says he met her in Ftan last night and that she's a mermaid. She is the City's queen, he explains, and invited him into her byssus palace, at the very heart of the tendrilled domain. He says he now understands everything, that he actually knew all along, and he berates himself for coming so many times to within a hair's breadth of the truth without being brave enough to accept it. He blames himself for being so stupidly unaware that all his dreams were calls, messages his mother sent him through the iguana. He says everything is beginning to make sense now that he has seen her, talked to her, that everything has become clear, that he finally knows who he really is. He is the result, he claims, of the involuntary union of that young royal mermaid and the Pig who caught her in his net one night. He is the hybrid fruit, the child of that loathsome embrace, whom his mortified mother reluctantly abandoned on the shore after his birth. He isn't Luc Bezeau, he tells me, but Fngl Mgl'Nf, the exiled prince of the Shimmering City, doomed to creep upon the earth among the plodders on account of those foreign genes that prevent him from living below the waves. But in the same breath he declares that this

185

will soon be put right and that his bitter, unnatural fate is already receding into the past, because the gliders are coming to get him — an escort has been dispatched by his mother to bring him back to her. He says they won't be long now, they should already be soaring over the Grand Banks, cleaving swiftly through the dark, phosphoric waters, and will soon be entering those of the Gulf. He tells me they will get here at the seventh tide and wait for him at the Île aux Oeufs, the island that used to have a lighthouse and is now a bird sanctuary in the middle of the river, miles away from anywhere. Luc says there will be magi among them who will be able to uncover his Ftan characteristics. They are going to teach him how to break out of the plodder chrysalis. They will assist him in his transformation. They will recompose his being and restore its aquatic essence. They are going to operate on him so he can breathe freely underwater. And then he will glide away with them, travel in their company beneath the surface of the ocean and join his mother. He swears it's all true, that he is going to Ftan, that Fngl will soon be returned to his people.

He is casting off the moorings. The rope of friendship he and I have twisted together still ties him to the world, but I can read in his hollow gaze that even this bond won't be able to hold him back much longer. Glider or not, he definitely needs a doctor, and I did my best to talk him into coming home with me, but I might as well have been pontificating into an echo chamber. Even Mama's message failed to sway him — he merely asked me to explain to her that he couldn't run the risk of getting caught, because he was to meet his own mother at a fixed time that couldn't possibly be changed. My friend is adrift. The worst of it is that he appears perfectly reasonable. He says he can understand my skeptical attitude. He admits it's all very hard to believe, that it sounds insane, and this is why he suggests I judge for myself — he wants me to go with him to the Île aux Oeufs. He wants me to see the gliders with my own eyes, to admire their powerful beauty, to find out that they are absolutely real. There, on the Île aux Oeufs, he'll say goodbye to me, but he quickly adds that there's no reason to be upset by this parting, because we are going to keep in touch thanks to the iguana. Besides, he'll often come to visit me in dreams, and also in person when he can, on days when spring tides surge against the shore.

He hovered in front of me, waiting for my answer, impatient to hear if I agreed to come to the island with him. For a brief moment I toyed with the idea of physically overpowering him, but my chances of success were so slim that I decided against it. I asked, instead, for a little time to think things over, and while he went off to play in the waves I consulted the iguana. I begged the lizard to intervene, to stop sending out at the very least those demented dreams that were creating such turmoil in my friend's mind. But the saurian merely smiled. A sphinx of the South Seas. A mangy Mona Lisa, will-o'-the-wisps dancing in her eyes.

* * *

In the tranquil silence of the cave, I felt my thinking becoming clearer and a conclusion presenting itself: since I could neither reason with Luc nor coerce him, I had to go to the island with him. I had to pretend I shared his delusion, play along with him.

* * *

I suggested to Luc we make a new pact: I would come along to the Île aux Oeufs and not stand in the way of him leaving with the mermen, provided he promised to return home with me without making a fuss if, for some reason or other, the water beings didn't show up. The arrangement suited him — that's how sure he was he would pull it off. And we clutched claws on that, performing the crab, mutually convinced we had clinched the deal of the century. It certainly was the *nuttiest* deal of the century.

* * *

I couldn't tell Mama in person because she wouldn't have let me leave again, so I went over to the house under cover of darkness and slipped a reassuring letter under the door in which I asked her to trust me and give me three more days. The first tide is ebbing. Now we only need to wait for the seventh.

29

Time flows lazily along at the Cove while Luc gets ready to leave. He has a lot to do. He began by sorting through the hundreds of notebook pages on which he'd scribbled his haiku in glider language, then he hurriedly finished his fresco, signing it with fluid hieroglyphs spelling out his name and rank in Ftanese. Now, he's preparing himself for the transformation and is totally engrossed with this approaching rebirth. He imprints the beach with unfamiliar dances — sinuous, ritual choreographies — then squats in his iguana crouch in the middle of the foreshore and meditates, singing throat songs that remind me of those of the Inuit.

Five more tides…

* * *

He is constantly awake, yet doesn't appear the least bit tired. Sleep passes him by, but in any case he no longer needs it to dream, because he is now so securely connected with the world of Ftan that all he has to do is close his eyes to get there. This is how he can track the journey of the queen's messengers, those awe-inspiring mermen speeding towards him with clouds of frightened plankton billowing in their wake. And at night, over the fire, he conjures up the cerulean mermaid who reigns over the swaying town. He translates for my benefit the sweet chats they have together. Then he'll wax lyrical again about the splendours of the City, its serpentine lanes vibrant with budding life, the peaceful ways and noble virtues of the aquatic nation. He makes it sound like the Garden of Eden and I'm getting caught up in it, believe in it — it's all so beautiful, so simple. I know perfectly well this whole glider thing is only poetry, fragile poetry, the chimerical invention of an unbridled imagination, but what good would it do to say this to him and start a useless argument? The near future will teach Luc that Ftan is merely a construct of his mind, and if we have to sail the swells all the way to the Île aux Oeufs for this, then off we go.

* * *

He has given me the iguana. Having to leave behind his old dream master saddened him, but how could he possibly take him along to where he is going? I promised to look after the lizard, but I'm wondering in fact what to do with him, since all he's been doling out to me lately are eerie, incomprehensible mirages in which penetrating bird's eyes alternate with sea-green visions of sunken ships. Could the dream machine be out of order? Overheated, perhaps, as a result of Luc's visionary bulimia? Anyhow, from now on I am responsible for the reptile, and Luc has strongly advised me to take excellent care of him, since he will soon be the only mental link between us.

* * *

With the rising of the fourth tide, the weather suddenly changed. The air thickened. The sky grew dim. The clouds began to seethe, the wind snapped at its own tail, and a storm broke — a mere prelude to a more terrible wrath. Fearing that his departure might be jeopardized, Luc stepped up to the edge of the hungry waves and improvised a frenzied mak-usham*. From the mouth of the cave, I could see him bellowing into the pandemonium and dancing in the downpour like a crazed faun. That galvanized gargoyle shrouded in sea spray hurled abuse at the convulsing elements, ordered them to cease their struggle and calm down, while flashes of lightning took his photograph. He roared terrible, blood-curdling pleas in the face of the chaos. He refused to yield, since his identity, even his very life, hung in the balance. At last, as the night wore on, he succeeded in driving the storm away. In its place a dense fog drifted over the weary sea, but Luc couldn't really complain since he had probably caused it himself by leaping about like that. A side effect.

Now, not a breath of wind rippled the ocean, but the weather remained unsettled. Luc felt it was too risky to wait. He meditated close to the iguana one last time, then gave the order to leave. Doubly protected by darkness and mist, we slipped out of the Cove and made our way to the beaches at Ferland. We still needed to solve our transportation problem since, on the map, the Île aux Oeufs rises out of the Gulf a good fifteen kilometres from the shore — a bit far for a swim. But Luc had planned ahead, and after leaving me to cool my heels all by myself for an hour in the thick soup that enveloped the old jetty at Pointe-Rouge, he came chugging towards me in his diver friends' Zodiac. I jumped aboard, choosing to believe he had permission to borrow that sacred skiff, and we disappeared into the bowels of the fog without so much as a compass to guide us.

30

Should gas bubbles invade the central nervous system (the brain and the spinal cord) — usually as a result of a diver's too rapid return to the surface — neurological decompression sickness will occur. This type of accident can be extremely serious if treatment isn't begun promptly.

It was teeming with birds. They were everywhere. High up on the bluffs and crammed into each pore of the island's brow were gulls and sterns, kingfishers, puffins, and some cormorant too. Even around us, they bobbed on the waves like decoys. We had come to a land inhabited by birds. No wonder it was called Île aux Oeufs — it must be swarming with eggs.

After meandering all day long through the fog, we were about to reach our destination. After oblivion, after the erratic north, after staring at the surface of that foam-flecked water, thinking we would drift on forever like lost astronauts, the Île aux Oeufs had suddenly emerged, right in front of the bow, looming out of the thick cotton wool like a mossy skull, so close already we almost bumped our noses. A Jurassic tortoise. King Kong's dead body off our shores. A giant lobster from the long-gone era before TV. Île aux Oeufs — our own, private Easter Island, a sliver of the Galápagos belonging to no one but us, the iguana's young disciples.

The strangest thing about the birds was their silence. Not a squawk rose into the air. Not a feather either, for that matter. The birds were dazed, stunned by the unusual sight of our arrival, amazed at our wingless audacity. But not at all intimidated, though. They didn't even move out of our way, floating about us like stupid bathtub toys we had to try and steer around. It looked as if they didn't want us to get through. The island itself was rugged, harsh, covered with tall, gullied forms. A mass of proud protrusions and faults, sitting haughtily on its viscous sides as though suddenly frozen in the middle of an upward thrust, a primordial surge, an effort to attack the horizontal stillness of the waters. We coasted over the reefs' crumbling fangs and other pitfalls cloaked in swirling seaweed. Dodging shoals and treacherous eddies, ignoring the round, wild bird's eyes that stripped our souls as we went by, we slipped past the island's western coast. And there, on a guano-speckled headland besieged by hordes of clawed and spluttering demons, we saw before us the tall, fog-ringed shape of the old lighthouse. It must have been ages since the melancholy leviathan's sweeping beam thrilled solitary rorquals; that pleasure had been stolen by the other skeleton-like robot, the hazy terminator towering a bit further away. But even if it was haunted now only by gulls and the ghosts of the drowned, that grim dungeon of the antisouth continued to stand.

The abandoned lighthouse was where we were bound, the appointed meeting place. At its base, a spit of grey sand was tenderly washed by the sea, and this is where we drew alongside it, wading through slimy water topped with shivery caps of froth. We didn't need to talk. We had nothing to say. While I tackled the job of setting up camp, Luc wandered off to explore the beach; then he perched on top of a slab of rock to smoke and read the weather. His clam face showed no emotion, but I could tell from the gleam in his Asiatic gaze that he was inwardly stamping his feet.

* * *

The sea has begun to rise, driving us back against the rocks. Now the day is giving way, the night creeping in. The fog won't let up. To distill its humours, I've lit a fire, which draws a dome of light from the impenetrable vapours, and while Luc paces back and forth I'm thinking about Mama who must be worried sick at the other end of the fog, and about my grand-folks who surely aren't attending to tomorrow's mail. I'd give anything to be with them right now in Grandmother's living room instead of here on this sinister, ocean-battered planet, but

I keep my spirits up by reminding myself that the loony odyssey is nearing its end. This very night we'll find out what value one should set on dreams and, at the first glimmerings of dawn, we will return to pedestrian reality. They'll be waiting for us. No doubt the police will have to be faced, and goodness knows what else. Will they be able to listen and understand? Are they going to be prepared to believe it's all the Pig's fault? Can those people who haven't been children for such a long time gauge the power of the golfer's enchantment? But tomorrow is a long way off for Luc, and he couldn't care less. He has more pressing concerns, such as controlling his impatience and searching the darkness on this whole crucial night of the seventh tide. Tomorrow is another world for Luc, another life.

Tired of roaming the beach like a restless werewolf, he has come and crouched down by the fire. He is all keyed up. He jumps at the faintest lap of the waves and continually trains his flashlight on the ocean. He lights one cigarette after another, the smoke coiling around his incandescent features, giving him an ephemeral mane. On this July night in my twelfth year, I am watching you, Luc Bezeau, and still can't figure you out — you exile, you proud Mongolian, you obstinate dreamer. You, my brother.

* * *

He was singing like an Inuit, filling our bubble of light with vibrations, and I contributed as best I could to the old, hypnotic refrain. It was a way of blotting out time and consciousness, of numbing the senses. The tension eased and I began to yawn non-stop, but just as I was about to zonk out, Luc left off singing, drew himself up, was on the qui vive. Stepping outside the fire's dazzling circle, he scanned the sea with his lamp. He mainly lit up the fog banks, but suddenly the light caught something. Forms were moving about at the surface. And a holy terror gripped me, because they were coming! Contrary to all expectations, the Ftan people were emerging, and their sleek bodies glistened at the gateway to our plodder world. But then, as I took a closer look, I realized I'd been taken in by the night's eerie mood — where I thought I'd seen a procession of mermen swimming into view, there were only branches sticking out of the water. A whole tree carried along by the tide, torn from a shore where no one claimed to have command over gales. Luc turned off his flashlight. He wandered back to the fire. He didn't feel like singing anymore.

A little while later, a south wind rose. It whipped up the sea and swept away the mist. Now, the night was clear, immaculate, and beneath the lucid glitter of the gemstones strewn about, it became difficult to believe in magic. The tide would never be higher. The hours' slope would soon reverse, and Luc was smoking away like an automaton. He was *so* anxious for something to happen he was about to explode.

* * *

It must have been about midnight when Luc heard the call. Like a murmur drifting on the waves. A trumpeting of conchs as well. I didn't pick up anything of the kind, but he insisted he clearly heard these sounds. Transfigured, he told me the water beings were there, just offshore, gathered on the seabed among wrecks of old warships, but weren't going to show themselves. Since they needed to be careful, they definitely wouldn't surface, but they were there waiting for him. They wanted him to come and meet them. And Luc was certainly not going to disappoint them. Actually, he had worked it all out beforehand: he jumped into the boat and lifted the cover of the locker. He took out a diving suit, Luigi's, with all the hardware. Flabbergasted, I stood watching him as he wriggled into the neoprene outfit and folded back the sleeves, which were too long. Then I pulled myself together, for he had to be stopped, and I tried to explain to him how dangerous it was to dive at night, especially for a beginner. I harped on it, I laid it on with a trowel, because I wanted him to understand and see reason. I assured him there weren't any conchs down there, let alone mermen, it was his imagination and

199

nothing else. But I was wasting my breath; I would have had better luck arguing with the sea itself. Luc put on his fins and fastened a serrated dagger to his leg, then he strapped his air tank to his back and I knew I wouldn't be able to keep him from leaving: his mother's messengers were waiting for him, and even his own fear wouldn't deter him. He said he had no choice, he had to go and see — if only to get to the bottom of it all. He had enough oxygen for one hour, he added, and promised to be back before it ran out. His cuttlefish eyes sparkled with excitement behind the glass pane of his mask. I stopped talking. His unbending will had defeated me.

He refused to be roped; he didn't want to be hindered in his movements in any way, and I made no attempt to rebel against this ultimate show of recklessness. Staggering along in his scuba gear, he stepped over the first waves and waded into the water until it reached his chest. Then he switched on his light and bit the mouthpiece. After a little wave in my direction, he melted into the ink, vanishing instantly. Now, there was only the blackness upon blackness of sky and water, that thick sandwich of gloom, that immense solitude. I felt utterly forlorn. I built up the fire with armfuls of dead wood — I wanted it to be big and boiling hot when my friend returned, because he would need all that warmth. But then I had a late reaction: it dawned on me that Luc would probably not come back. And I was overcome by fear, the kind of fear that starts at your extremities and sweeps through you, chilling your blood. I decided to act, to go in search of Luc right away, and I pushed the boat into the waves. I didn't dare use the motor for fear of hitting my friend or tearing him to shreds, so I rowed away from the shore instead. As I leaned over the gunwale, my eyes sounded the black, heaving mass of the waves, while the oxygen drained away minute by precious minute.

The wind grew stronger, deepened the swell, shifted mountains of darkness, and my skiff shrank beneath me, seeming frailer and frailer. I didn't have a watch, but didn't need one to know that the hour had passed. Yet I continued to X-ray the visceral expanse of the waters, still hoping Luc would suddenly appear. And just as I was going to give up and return to the island, my perseverance paid off: a glint of moonlight revealed a bright object about a hundred fathoms away. I started up the engine and made straight for that yellow thing floating on the swell; it was the inflated vest of Luc's diving suit.

He was like a drowned wasp. Lifeless. Unconscious. I hauled him aboard, not without difficulty since he weighed as much as a halibut. I took off his mask. He was breathing, but there was blood flowing from his nostrils. I settled him at the bow, then headed for the shore at full throttle. Ferland lay to the north. I found the Big Dipper, followed the Pole Star. At last, I spotted the lights of our village, that dotted line of low stars along the water's edge, and I aimed at the centre of that flat galaxy, where

Dr. Lacroix's house stood. We were still quite a distance from the shore when Luc regained consciousness. He was confused, shivering, but still strong enough to rebel when he found out where we were going. As if he'd been electrocuted. He ordered me to do a U-turn. He wanted me to take him back to the Île aux Oeufs and drop him off in the water again. When I refused, he became excited, squirmed like a garter snake. Suddenly, with unexpected vigour, the impossible son-of-a-screwball jumped overboard, this time without a safety vest. I cursed, turned around, and managed to catch him by the hair just as he was about to go under. Fishing him out yet again put me out of breath, but he, on the other hand, seemed in better shape than before. He was wide-awake now. Alert. His dive had settled him down. He no longer demanded we return to the island. He only wanted us to go to the Cove and, since he really did seem to be better, I accepted this compromise. Gripping the tiller, I propelled our expedition like a fat bumblebee towards the sombre heights of the Gigots.

As soon as the boat ran aground on the sand at the Cove, I realized I had underestimated the seriousness of Luc's condition. He was paralysed on the spot, unable to move. I had to help him out of the Zodiac. His legs buckled under him and he collapsed, knifed by violent cramps. I regretted I hadn't stuck to my initial plan. I suggested I take him over to the doctor's place but he wouldn't hear of it and started

202

crawling on his elbows towards the cave. I carried him inside and laid him down beside the iguana. The cramps seemed to be easing off. They came on less frequently, anyway, so he was able to enjoy a few moments' respite. But ten minutes later he was feverish, haunted by hallucinations, and began to rave out loud. He said that down below, on the ocean floor, he had seen the water beings from Ftan with their gleaming lances of mother-of-pearl, that he'd swum in search of them among the barnacle-covered wrecks and finally found those graceful manatees, sheathed in shimmering light. They had formed a luminous circle around him and greeted him with reverence, then they'd bent over him and performed their surgical magic. That's why he was having those cramps, all that pain. They were the first signs of his metamorphosis. His body was going to be transformed, his true nature revealed, and it was the kind of change that couldn't happen without suffering. He was so tired his eyes had sunk deep into their sockets. He escaped into a seismic sleep, murmuring in the language of mermaids. As far as I could judge, he was talking to his mother.

* * *

The dawn's pointed fingers were probing the cave's bowels and tickling my lashes. Outside, there were at least a million screeching gulls, but what really woke me up were Luc's groans. He was in a bad way. He writhed, moaned, trembled all over. His nose was bleeding. His left eye was a scarlet ball. He could no longer move. He couldn't even talk anymore. But he was still able to click his teeth, and it was in Morse code that he told me not to be afraid: Metamorphosis — Not really dying — Changing — Take Zodiac back — Hug your mother for me — Take care iguana — I love you — Drop me off in the water — In the open sea — Is necessary for completion of metamorphosis — Don't forget — Important — Thank you my friend — Goodbye.

His arched limbs jerked uncontrollably. His body really did seem to be trying to change shape, to contort itself in order to adopt a new configuration, yet a smile lit up his face, made him look almost handsome. His breathing became irregular and I understood that life was draining from him, expelled with each convulsive movement as from a cut artery. I bolted from the cave to get the boat ready, fill up the gas tank, and spread out life jackets to form a makeshift bed. This is when the silence struck me. The gulls had stopped squawking. Perched all along the nearby ledges, they were eyeing me. I jumped when the first one flapped its wings and flew away. It was followed by another one, then a third, a fourth, and within seconds the whole flock had scattered all over the sky. I stood watching them for a while as they faded into the distance, then I went back into the cave. I already knew Luc's suffering was over.

He had broken free. He had found peace. Eyes wide open, he gazed up at the rocky ceiling that portrayed the splendours of Ftan. He looked utterly amazed. He seemed to have been transported right into the heart of an extraordinary vision, a dream so sublime that dying from it was justified.

* * *

I let the day go by so as to be really sure. I waited till dusk, then began to carry out his last wish. I dressed him in his wacky best, tied his favourite strings of seashells and bracelets to his arms and legs, then I wrapped him together with the iguana in a shroud of living seaweed. It was the kind of night he would have enjoyed — balmy, perfect, illuminated by a gigantic moon and skimmed by a breeze that barely puckered the smooth skin of the waters. It was an offering from the tropics, a tribute they paid him; if a reflection of mangroves had appeared in the bay, I wouldn't have been the least bit surprised. I laid Luc down in the Zodiac, negotiated the reefs, and headed south.

When I'd reached the open sea, I cut the motor. And once the boat had coasted to a stop, I relieved Luc of his plodder weight. He slipped overboard, rippling the night sky that glittered in the jet-black mirror, but he didn't go under right away. He suddenly wasn't in such a hurry to dive anymore. He floated for a while, dawdling at the edge of both worlds, then slowly sank, head first, as though in memory of the *Titanic*. I plunged a waterproof flashlight below the surface to track his languid falling-leaf descent. As he spiralled down, it was as if he swayed in iridescent oil teeming with shadowy forms. The tropical sun wasn't going to bleach his bones after all. They would adorn the briny depths instead. They would decorate some moray's lair, and it was right that it should be this way. It seemed fitting that when all was over for Luc he could fulfill his wish to disappear into the ocean and join the mother he had tried so desperately to find. The darkness finally swallowed him up. I switched off my lamp but remained bent over the waves. Perhaps I hoped to catch another kind of light, a glow that would have penetrated the waters' intimate secret, a phosphorescence rising from the depths to welcome my friend. But there was nothing emanating from the deep. The wondrous event wasn't going to take place.

And yet... A little later, as I lay sleeping in the cave for the last time, I dreamt about Luc. I saw him drifting down towards the bottom of the ocean while throngs of sand eels undulated by his side and fed on him. Like gentle piranhas, they nibbled him, gnawed into his flesh, sculpting it with their tiny teeth. They were remodelling Luc's body, giving it a new, pure, streamlined form. I heard a harmonic murmur, a low, powerful chorus, and now I really saw that abyssal luminescence rising from the depths. An underwater comet flared out of the gloom, escorted by whales, octopuses, and harnessed sharks ridden by singing water beings from the Great Medusa.

Rejoice, mermaids and mermen. Yes, sing below the waves, you denizens of the deep, for Fngl Mgl'Nf is here. Greet him with cheers, all you gliders. Sound his praises. Blow the conchs. The Prince of the Shimmering City has finally returned.

Translator's Note to Page 187

* *Makusham:* a ceremonial feast including drum dances, which used to be held after the hunt by the Innu (also called Montagnais-Naskapi), the Aboriginal inhabitants of the eastern and northern portions of the Quebec-Labrador Peninsula.

About the Author

Denis Thériault is an award-winning author and screenwriter living in Montreal, Canada. His much-loved novels *The Peculiar Life of a Lonely Postman* and *The Postman's Fiancée* (Oneworld, 2017) have enjoyed international success. First published in Canada in 2003, *The Boy Who Belonged to the Sea* is his debut novel.

About the Translator

Liedewy Hawke's translation *Hopes and Dreams: The Diary of Henriette Dessaulles, 1874–1881* won the 1986 Canada Council Prize for Translation (now the Governor General's Literary Award for Translation) as well as the John Glassco Translation Prize. Her other translations include *Memoria* (Dundurn Press, 1999), *House of Sighs* (The Mercury Press, 2001), and *The Milky Way* (Dundurn Press, 2002), which was shortlisted for the 2002 Governor General's Literary Award for Translation.

Oneworld, Many Voices

Bringing you exceptional writing
from around the world

The Woman at 1,000 Degrees by Hallgrímur Helgason
(Icelandic) Translated by Brian FitzGibbon

Frankenstein in Baghdad by Ahmed Saadawi (Arabic)
Translated by Jonathan Wright

Back Up by Paul Colize (French)
Translated by Louise Rogers Lalaurie

Damnation by Peter Beck (German)
Translated by Jamie Bulloch

Oneiron by Laura Lindstedt (Finnish)
Translated by Owen Witesman

The Boy Who Belonged to the Sea by Denis Thériault
(French) Translated by Liedewy Hawke

The Baghdad Clock by Shahad Al Rawi (Arabic)
Translated by Luke Leafgren

The Aviator by Eugene Vodolazkin (Russian)
Translated by Lisa C. Hayden

Lala by Jacek Dehnel (Polish)
Translated by Antonia Lloyd-Jones